I0718461

Felix Publishing 2021
email: info.felixpublishing@gmail.com
Print copies available from publisher.

The Confessions of Father Xavier

Print Edition
ISBN: 978-1-925662-40-5
Digital Edition
ISBN: 978-1-925662-41-2
Author: Dr Peter T. Scott (as Hernán Eduardo Moreno Ruiz)

Registration:
Thorpe-Bowker +61 3 8517 8342
email: bowkerlink@thorpe.com.au

This is a work of fiction. The characters in this book did not exist and the politics of the time has been generalized. Some of the places described are real and are well-known to the author. No disrespect is meant to any people living or dead in the countries of South America for which the author has a great love.

The Confessions
Of
Father Xavier

Hernán Moreno Ruiz

MAR CARIBE
MAPA 1
COLOMBIA
Quito
Baños
ECUADOR
Guayaquil
Iquitos
MAP 2
BRAZIL
PERU
Lima
Cuzco
Andes
La Paz
BOLIVIA
Altiplano
PARAGUAY
OCÉANO PACÍFICO
CHILE
Pampas
URUGUAY
Buenos Aires
Mercedes
ARGENTINA
ANDES
OCÉANO ATLÁNTICO
Tierra del Fuego
Ushuaia
SUDAMERICA
1870
SCALE 1:35,000,000

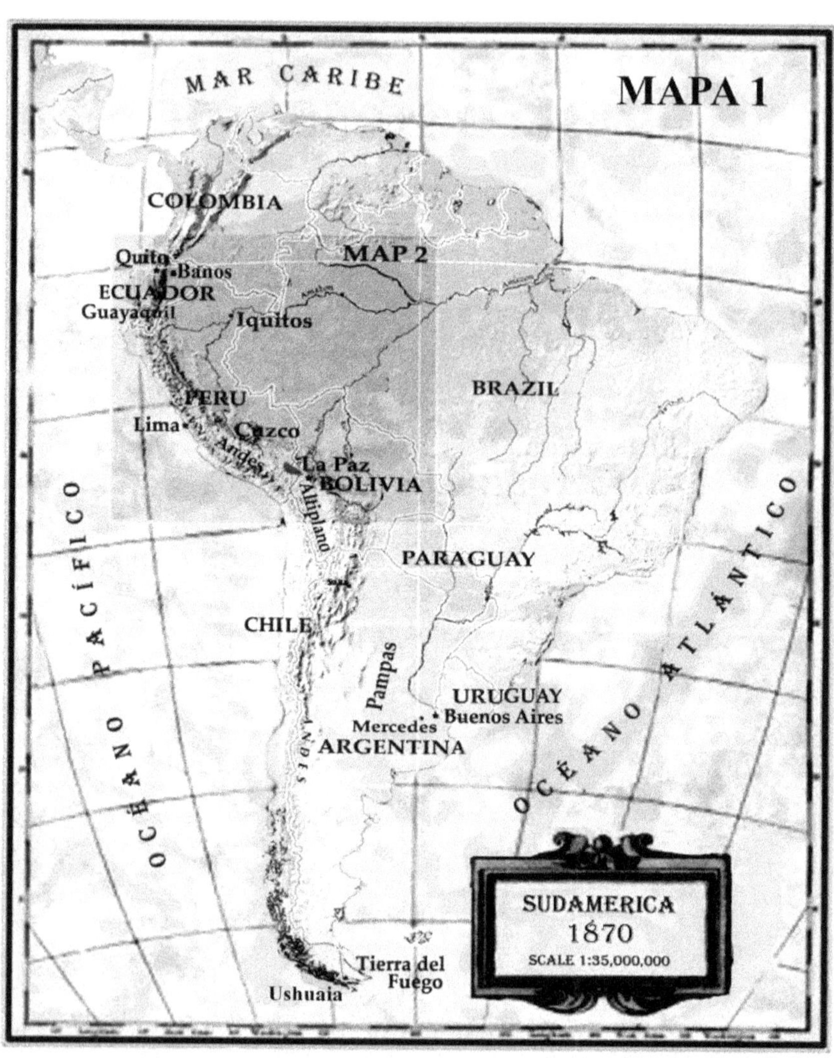

iv

MAPA 2
COLOMBIA
ECUADOR
Quito
Ambato
Banos
Riobamba
Guayaquil
Zarumilla
Cuenca
Rio Pastaza
Rio Marañon
Iquitos
Rio Amazonas
PERU
BRAZIL
Trujillo
Huarmey
Rio Madre de Dios
Lima
Cuzco
Huancane
Lago Titicaca
Juliaca
Puno
Copacabana
Arequipa
La Paz
BOLIVIA
0   1000
km

To my grandchildren who are yet
to find their own adventures.

Contents

Introduction

There are some memories which fade with age; but those which are important to one's soul survive.

It was the start of the new decade of the new century and I was cleaning out my desk of my study in the Universidad Nacional de San Antonio. The weather had been warm for January but there was a cold wind blowing from the northwest off the snows of Sallqantay. I walked over to my open casement window, closed it and secured its latch when there was a knock at the door.

"Enter!" I called out. The door was of a heavy wood panelling as was befitting the building which dated from the seventeenth century.

Sergio, the faculty's general factotum whom I had known for many years and now was stooped with age slowly opened the heavy door and entered the room. He still wore his faded jacket and undergraduate gown favoured by many of the university's non-academic staff.

"Buenos días, Don Hernán," he said with the same enigmatic smile which he always seemed to have, and gave his usual small formal bow. "Here is a letter and a package for you" he continued.

I rushed across the room and took the large package from the old servant for it was heavy and Sergio had struggled with it as he had entered. It was tightly wrapped in old brown leather and tied securely with a thin hempen rope.

"There is a letter, also" he said, reaching under his gown and into the pocket of his equally faded brown pantaloons. Sergio had long since reached retirement age but had continued to work to support his grandchildren of whom he was very proud. I felt somewhat ashamed that I was retiring at a much younger age and could now go on to continue my study interest in the ancient Greek warrior-philosophers in the comfort of my home. Of course, I had been offered the honorary post of Professor Emeritus in the Faculty of Philosophy and would continue to wander around its colonnaded quadrangles and the library with its book-covered walls and ancient wooden tables.

"We will be sad to see you go, Don Hernán." Sergio said quietly as he closed the heavy door behind him.

Ignoring the package, I opened the letter. It was contained in a large envelope which bore the emblem of the Society of Jesus[1] on its reverse side.

---

[1] The Society of Jesus, commonly known as 'the Company' or simply as Jesuits.

I walked to my window and looked out across the narrow lane to the brown stone walls of the Jesuit church[2] with its Baroque architecture and its ornate bell towers to the Plaza de Armas[3] beyond. At the end of the lane, across the plaza, I could see the dark green of the low, rounded hills which surround the city of Cuzco here in the high mountains of Peru.

The emblem brought back many memories of my friendship with the Jesuit Father Xavier; that most generous but secretive of men who I had first met almost twenty years ago when Garcia and I had returned to San Rafael. I now realised with some shock that the envelope was edged in black and I tore it open with some trepidation. The letter read:

---

[2] Iglesia de la Compañía de Jesús (Church of the Society of Jesus)

[3] 'Weapons Square', but better translated as Parade Square so given by the early Spanish conquerors but now used to signify the main square of many Hispanic American cities or towns.

"It is with some regret and considerable personal sadness that I must tell you of the passing of our beloved brother and friend Father Xavier.

He died peacefully in his sleep in our Residence in Lima and was interned in our vault in the Basilica of San Pedro, here in Lima.
He was my particular friend and mentor. You might remember me as the shy student who travelled with the good father and you and your friends on the coach to Copacabana those many years ago. You may recall that I had said that I was travelling to San Pablo de Tiquina to visit my uncle and that was the truth. In reality I must confess that Father Xavier had asked me to travel with you, to see if you and your companions had ventured past Copacabana and on to La Paz. Here he would have had other contacts to meet the coach. Father Xavier was a most wonderful man and had friends in many parts of our continent.

We Jesuits are not men of great wealth and usually have little property, but Father Xavier was not typical of most of our order. Against the usual practice, he kept diaries, secret to all who knew him except those of his closest confidence. I was lucky to be considered one of these and when I joined the order, he became my mentor where I often assisted him in some of his work in upholding the Faith and caring for our indigenous brothers.

On his deathbed, he asked me to send you all of his diaries in the hope that you may use them as an illustration and in the service of the poor.

I hope that I may also be counted as your friend,

Father Diago Ramírez Ortiz SJ
Lima, 1910.

So it was that I learned of the passing of my good friend Father Xavier. A man of prodigious intellect, reasoning and care for his fellow man. Truly a man of God but also one who could move in the circles of power here on Earth and who was the confidante of many in high office. Whilst I had been an 'Exploring Officer' in the intelligence service of my country and had openly searched for our enemies, Father Xavier had travelled in a darker country of intrigue and espionage which was much more dangerous.

I bent down and lifted the heavy package onto my desk. With my knife, which, out of force of habit I kept in my boot, I cut open the rope and unfolded the leather covering. Contained therein were several large notebooks; the kind of which people would jot down their daily events and thoughts. These were Father Xavier's diaries.

They were numbered in a neat script and I opened the first. It was written in Father Xavier's strong, neat hand, using an economy of words typical of a man of such intellect and science.

It was fascinating reading and I knew from his character that he would want others to know of his story. I put aside my thoughts of studying the warrior-philosophers of ancient Greece and decided to study a more modern counterpart.

So, with the hope that I would have his blessings from Heaven, I have used his diaries to outline in narrative form, the life and adventures of my good friend, Father Xavier.

Hernán Eduardo Moreno Ruiz
Cuzco, January 10th 1910.

Capítulo Uno:
La Muerte de Un Alma
(Chapter One: The Death of a Soul)

Xavier Aguirre del Rio, Capitán de Tropa[1] of the 23rd Hussars sheathed his heavy cavalry sabre into its scabbard and dismounted. As usual, his Troop Sargent, Manuel, was at hand to take the reins of his horse Kiyari[2].

He slowly walked a few steps into the plaza of the small village of Huancané which stood on the northern shores of Lake Titicaca and took off his kepi[3]. Tears filled his eyes.

Before him lay the bodies of many of the villagers; men mostly, although several of them appeared to be no more than boys. There were a few women also in their tangled skirts, clustered around the dry,

---

[1] Troop Captain – in charge of a troop of cavalry, about 100 men

[2] "Moonlight" in the Quechua language.

[3] Kepi – a military cap with a horizontal peak.

central fountain where they had tried to seek refuge.

He looked around at the buildings which fronted the plaza; the small, adobe church on one side and the two-story building with its limp and partly torn wiphala – that square flag of coloured diagonal checks of the native peoples of the Andes – which was the office of the Alcalde[4]. He had been too late.

"Teniente Alonso" he called, turning back to his troop. "Take your men and scout around the outskirts of the village. Report back to me if you find any of the villagers alive." It was grim task.

"Dismount and find some shade," he called back to the remainder of the troop. He sat down on a nearby kerbstone and rubbed his face with his kepi. What had happened here?

---

[4] Mayor

His regiment had dispatched his troop to this village of Huancané in support of other units and the militia who had been sent to supress the local population. Not many years previously, a prominent merchant and rich landowner, Juan Bustamante Dueñas, who had also been an elected Prefect of the district of Puno, had taken up the plight of the local indigenous people. At the request of the Hacendados – those rich owners of large estates who often exploited the local people as indentured farm laborers - the government had sent an army under the command of General Baltazar Caravedo. But Caravedo had been an honourable man and refused to attack the local people, preferring dialogue instead. Bustamante had reached an agreement with General Caravedo, who then withdrew with his troops to Lima. The landowners accused Caravedo of complicity with the indigenous people and again hostilities broke out with the indigenous people and so Xavier's troop was called out.

By the time he had arrived with his Troop, many old scores had obviously been settled and the people once more suppressed.

Teniente Alonso returned, his face set in grim mask.

"Capitán Aguirre, please would you come with me. I have something to show you which our troopers should not see."

The captain mounted his horse and followed his Lieutenant down a narrow street which led out of the centre of the village. Not far they came to a single tall tree, an uncommon sight here in the altiplano. Hanging by its heels from one of its most prominent branches was the corpse of a headless man. The head lay at some distance, the dead eyes staring up to the sky.

"Cut that thing down!" The Captain ordered the Sergeant who had been standing guard near the tree, his sabre over his right shoulder. "And place the body near its head."

This being done, the captain rode over and looked at the corpse. Its body was dressed like that of a country gentleman in a dark frock coat and the head had been placed as neatly as could be arranged by the Sergeant who was about to cover its eyes with a handkerchief.

"Wait!" the Captain said, leaning over from his saddle and looking at the body below him. "That is the remains of Juan Bustamante Dueñas, the patriot and reformer. What a dreadful way to die!"

He turned his horse back towards the village. "Cover his eyes, now Sergeant. I will send some troopers back to help with his burial."

Back with the troop, the Captain remounted his horse just as a small group of men emerged from the church across the plaza. Its leader was taller than most of the other men and he wore a faded red sash across his broad chest. Whilst the other held back, the leader walked slowly up to the Captain, his broad black hat held in both hands. He looked up at the tall officer in his fine uniform mounted on an equally fine chestnut horse and said in a trembling voice:

"Forgive us señor, but you see what has been done to our people!" he said sadly, spreading his arms around at the scene behind him. "Do you want to kill all of us? We have made our confessions in the church and are ready to die as a free people."

The Captain looked down with sorrow in his heart and tears in his eyes. He dismounted, removed his kepi and walked up to the Alcade.

"Forgive me, Señor Alcade. This was neither our doing nor our want. I was sent here to support the devils who did this, but I am sure that my men would not attack a defenceless village. We were told only that there was a rebel army in this area and to give support."

The Alcade spat onto the dry ground and looked up at the Captain who was still much taller than him. "Support! Bah! Murder you mean?"

The Captain looked across the plaza where the people were beginning to look for loved ones amongst the corpses.

"I too am deeply saddened by what has happened here. You see those women near the fountain? In a time gone by, one of them could have been my grandmother, Doña Kantuta Aguirre Mamani. So! I weep with you and your people!" The Captain's anger subsided and tears once more came to his eyes.

The Alcade lowered his eyes and quietly replied:

"I am sorry, señor. The name of Mamani is still know in this village. Once a great family but no more because of the greed of the Hacendados. Forgive me. I will return to my people and we will get on with the burying of our dead."

The Captain turned to Teniente Alonso who was standing quietly by his side.

"Have the men fall out and help these poor people bury the dead and send four troopers back to that tree to bring the body back here to his people for burial. There is nothing more here for us."

Having returned to his regiment at Juliaca, the Captain went directly to his quarters and sat on his bed staring at nothing in particular. His mind was in turmoil trying to find the meaning of his profession as a soldier. He had imagined that he would be the country's protector against its enemies, not against the poor, downtrodden peons of his grandmother's people.

That night he slept a restless sleep. In his disturbed mind he revisited that fatal plaza with its pitiful corpses of villagers. He had fond but distant memories of his grandmother, but he imaged in his dream that all of the corpses in the square were like her; older women wearing their traditional polleras or wide skirts, made from handwoven alpaca wool with a broad lliclla shawl around their necks. He woke with a sudden gasp of air and, despite the cool of the morning was covered in sweat.

He washed, dressed and went to the Officers' Mess as usual, but he found the food generally unappetising and he was unaware of the friendly salutations and conversation of his brother officers. He returned to his room and thought more about his predicament; silently going over the words which he would reluctantly need to say later that morning. Eventually, he came to the only conclusion that he could possibly come to and so he left his quarters and walked over to the main building across the parade ground.

"Is the Colonel in?" He asked the Regimental Adjutant, taking off his kepi. As usual, the Adjutant was busy at his desk in the outer office of the headquarters building sorting out some papers. Capitán Martínez looked up from the pile of papers through which he was rummaging and smiled at his friend:

"Buenos días, Xavier! Yes. He is in and for once seems to be in a good mood." He stood up, knocked once on the heavy oaken door and looked in.

"Capitán Aguirre to see you, sir." He announced and stood aside as he opened the door to let his brother officer pass.

Xavier gave a slight smile but was dreading this moment. "Thank you, Francisco" he said as he walked through the opened doorway.

"Ah, Aguirre! Come in, I just have one more tedious document to sign. I have read your report of the Huancané incident. Nasty business. Sit down won't you?"

The young captain came to the position of attention, his kepi still in his hand. "Thank you, sir but I will stand if you don't mind."

The Colonel looked up slightly flustered at this formal reply. He liked this tall officer and had always put formalities aside when speaking with him. For his part, Xavier knew the Colonel as a hard but fair superior who always had time for his men. At times he would be sharp at his response to perceived incompetence, no matter how slight, and the troopers were always at their best when Coronel Molina was on one of his many inspections. The Colonel put down his pen and looked up at his young subordinate.

"Well, Xavier. What is the matter?" he asked. "Is it about Huancané?"

"Yes sir."

"Well." The Colonel hesitated a little, looking down again at the papers on his desk. "In retrospect, had I known that you had a personal connection to the area, I would not have assigned your troop to assist the Hacendados. Your grandmother's people you said in your report?"

"Yes sir."

"I am sorry. I cannot use the excuse that such action came down from Lima as a direct order, which it did, but I should have been more aware of your sensitivities. So, how can I help you now?"

"I am sorry, too Coronel, but I feel that such an event may become more common in this part of Peru and so I wish to reign my Commission."

"Resign your Commission, Xavier?" the Colonel said with some surprise standing up. "I did not expect that! You are one of my best officers and tacticians! One of the best horsemen I have seen in years and the Regimental fencing champion to boot. Please consider what you have just asked me."

"I too am sorry, sir, but I feel that I could not do my duty to the best of my ability after being at Huancané. I would see our role as being the suppression of the local people and in support of the rich land-owners."

The colonel sat down and wiped his brow with a handkerchief which he produced from his sleeve. He looked up again at the young Captain.

"Perhaps you are right, Xavier. We are soldiers and do the bidding of our political masters. They start the mess and we have to clean it up! I truly am sorry about your grandmother's people for it is they we swore to protect when we took our oath at the Academy. Family is more important than politics. Blood is thicker than the wine of the stateroom."

Coronel Molina stood up and walked around his desk to where the young captain was standing. He put his arm around the young man's shoulder and said quietly:

"You know. Your good father, the Colonel, is not going to approve of your decision. I knew him when I was one of his students at the Academy. We were always in fear of him!" he said with a little laugh.

"Thank you, sir. I think that you are right. He had the same effect on us when we were children but I hope that he has mellowed over these past years since our mother died."

"Well, I hope that you are right. Never-the-less, I will write to him and try to explain your feelings. But he will take it hard, I think. I will reluctantly accept your resignation; Capitán Martínez will see to all of the formalities. When do you propose to leave us?"

"As soon as I can, Colonel. There will be a coach going to Arequipa at the end of the week and from there I should make the connection to Matarani and take ship to Lima"

"That is the best way." The Coronel replied. "Even a good horseman such as yourself would find the coach trip to Lima a long and arduous journey. At least this way will give a sea voyage which might clear up your thoughts, huh!

"Thank you for your understanding, sir." The young captain said, bringing his heels together in a smart position of attention.

With nothing more to be said, he turned quickly on his heels and walked out of the room, closing the door gently behind him.

"No problems with the Colonel, Xavier?" his friend the Adjutant asked.

"No, he was very understanding" there was a long embarrassing pause. "Francisco…. I have resigned my Commission." He confessed.

The Adjutant put down his pen and looked up at his friend with some disbelief. "Xavier! But why?"

Xavier, his kepi still in his hand and his head hanging low slowly explained his reasons to his friend who sat for a while in silence when he had finished.

"Well, we will be sad to see you go. You have been a good friend and the men all think highly of you, but I understand. My mother's people come from the south of the lake, near Puno they were there before the Spaniards arrived, so you see I can share some of your pain."

"Thank you, Francisco. I will remember you and the regiment with fondness. Adiós!"

With that, he turned, replaced his kepi and left the room. Walking across the parade ground he thought of all of the good times which he had experienced in his regiment which he was about to leave; his comrades and the many parades in the town during fiestas. He thought of his horse Kiyari, and walked across to the stable where she was housed along with the other horses of the regiment. He would miss her as there was a strong bond between most cavalrymen and their horses. She was on the entitlement of the regiment, but like most of the officers, he had purchased her himself from a good horse stud north of the town. She had been an excellent mount and always seemed to be aware of his moods and was responsive to his every command. He would miss her but would give her to his friend Francisco. The Adjutant came from a poor family and could not afford to buy his own horse and besides, Xavier knew that his friend would care for Kiyari as he would himself.

Very early next morning, he left the barracks quietly dressed in civilian clothes, walking out of the gate to the bemused salute of the sentry. It was but a short distance to the coaching inn where he purchased a ticket for the morning coach which would take him down the long, dusty mountain road to the city of Arequipa. Here he found lodgings at the Posada Nueva España in the respectable barrio del Yanahuara[5], a family inn where he had once stayed several years previously on another journey home.

He had always liked this city, with its impressive view of the great Volcán El Misty which dominated the region. Here the people were friendly and there was a nice

---

[5] The New Spain Inn in the neighbourhood of Yanahuara in northern Arequipa. The Yanahuara – 'the tribe who wore black shorts' who once lived there.

restaurant upstairs near the Cathedral in the Plaza de Armes. In a happier time, he would have stayed for a few days and enjoyed the sights and hospitality of its people but now he continued his journey to the sea port of Matarani where he would take passage on to Lima.

The voyage would take only about five days as the steamer would use its auxiliary sails and the assistance the Southeast Trade winds. Xavier spent most of his time alone in his cabin or walking the deck late at night, for even with the fresh sea air, he found sleeping difficult. At the table he tried to keep out of social conversation and when this was impossible to do, he played the lonely part of an officer returning home to some sad family tragedy for this is what he truly expected.

On the last day, the steamer rounded the northern tip of the Isla San Lorenzo and docked at its port in the Callao District.

Xavier took leave of the ship's captain and walked down the gangway to the many carriages for hire waiting on the dock. He took a small trap[6] the few kilometres to the wealthy district not far from the centre of the city where the family mansion stood. He paid the driver, picked up his bag and walked across the street to the large, ornate doors which formed the entrance to the inner courtyard. He rang the bell which hung to one side and a small wicket door opened to reveal the stern face of Joaquín, his father's manservant and former batman.

"Why, Don Xavier!" the old soldier exclaimed with a sudden smile. "Come in, young sir. "He opened the small door wider so that Xavier could enter." Your father is probably in the library at this hour, Don Xavier. I will take your bag to your old room and make it ready."

---

[6] A trap is a light, two-wheeled horse-drawn carriage

Xavier walked into the outer courtyard with its reception rooms and stables and through the small archway into the inner courtyard. Here was once the beautiful garden and fountain which his mother had tended with such love and in which she had told stories to him and his younger siblings under the lemon tree near the central fountain. Now the garden was but a faint remnant of his former beauty. The fountain was no longer sparkling with water and the lemon tree hung bare of leaves and fruit. The tiled pathways were now overgrown with weeds as was the rest of the garden.

Xavier walked through the open doorway which led into the main part of the building and into the library. His father, Coronel Roberto Aguirre del Rio y Montoya stood at the window thumbing through a large book, he turned sharply when he heard his son enter.

"Xavier! Well, this is a surprise" he said without much change on his stern face. "I did not expect you home from leave at this time of year!" He put the book down and came closer to his son. "You are wearing civilian clothing. What is the meaning of this?" he said with some suspicion in his eyes.

Xavier, even as a former captain in the army of Peru was still afraid of his father but truth was always his only way.

"I have resigned my commission, father," was all that he could say, "did you not get a letter from Coronel Molina?"

"Resigned your commission?" the older man looked at his son, his stern face reddened and his hands clenching at his side. "What letter? The mails from Juliaca have always been slow. What do you mean by resigning your commission?"

Xavier took a step forward towards his father, his hand out in a gesture of peace but his father suddenly turned away and walked back to the window. "I suppose you have a good reason for such a disgraceful action?" he father angrily said. "Our family have always held high positions in the army and you are the first to reject your responsibility. Explain!" he said, turning once more to his son.

Xavier stood where he was and in a quiet voice explained the horror, he had experienced at Huancané and his feelings of sorrow towards his grandmother's people. He heard himself speak like he had never spoken to his father before; he was not sorry for resigning his commission as it was a matter of honour that he could no longer serve an army which killed its own people.

His father listened in stern silence and then walked up to his son. His face full of anger, he said.

"Honour! It is no honour for an officer to resign his commission! You have disgraced your family! Your mother, if she were alive today, would probably say something different! But her mother is also long gone, so you were defending no one's honour! It is a good thing that your brother and sister are not here! You are no son of mine and there is no place for you here!"

The old man turned sharply and walked back to the window, turning his back on his son.

Xavier stood for a moment, stunned at his father's reaction to his news. He knew from past experience that any further explanation would simply increase the tension of the moment; his father always had a talent for using destructive argument.

With nothing further to say, Xavier left the room and slowly climbed the stairs to his old room, tears welling up in his eyes. There he found Joaquín repacking his bag.

"Forgive me Don Xavier, but it was difficult not to over hear the Colonel's rebuke." There was little in the house that Joaquín did not hear. Even as a boy, Xavier had found that this genial old man was always one step in front of the actions of himself and his siblings. Joaquín was the perfect manservant; always there when needed and always with a solution to the most difficult of problems.

"I have taken the liberty of hanging your uniforms in your closet and have replaced them with some fresh civilian clothing; some fresh shirts and your travelling coat as well."

"Thank you, Joaquín. That was most astute of you, but tell me, where is my sister Gabriella?"

The old man looked up and smiled:

"Doña Gabriella is staying with another young lady from her school for the weekend, but she will be home on Monday, Don Xavier. Will you wait for her return?"

"Alas, no, Joaquín. Considering my father's mood, I think that I should leave as soon as I can. I will write a short note of explanation to her, if you will ask your good wife to hand it to her when she returns."

"Thank you, Don Xavier. I am sure that my Maria will do so with the most delicacy as she does with caring for your father and his house."

"And please give Señora Maria my thanks for her care of my father and of myself and my siblings. Especially after our mother died," he added with sadness in his heart.

"Don Xavier," Joaquín said quietly coming closer to the young man. "If you would permit some advice from an old soldier, perhaps it would be advisable to 'make a tactical withdrawal' as you officers would say? I am sure that your father, the Colonel, will come to his senses in time."

"Thank you, Joaquín. Perhaps you are right. I will leave quietly and hope that he will see that the resignation of my commission was the only honourable thing that I could have done under the circumstances.

"I am sure that he will, Don Xavier," the old man replied. "As the family is well-known here in Lima, perhaps you could seek some shelter elsewhere, if I may be so bold as to suggest this also."

"Yes, you are right, my father has too many friends in this city, so I will travel and see what the world has to offer. I will write to my brother Alejandro when I can. I would not like to affect his studies at the Military Academy. Thank you Joaquín for your kindness and wise council."

"Thank you, Don Xavier, I wish you good fortune in your life." With that the old man gave a small bow and quietly left the room

Capítulo Dos:
Éxodo al Desierto
(Chapter Two: Exodus into the Desert)

It was difficult to leave the big house in which he, his sister and young brother had known laughter and happiness in his early days as a child. He felt alone and very vulnerable as he quietly closed the rear door of the house and walked down the narrow path to the road. The sweet smell of the row of mauve Mirabilis flowers growing along the side wall was the only sensation which he now experienced.

Xavier closed the small gate at the side of the house and turned into the quiet street. He was oblivious to the direction he was walking; he simply walked, his head full of the consequences of his recent conversation with his father. He was conscious that he was now walking down the Jirón Callao, that narrow street with its many colonnaded shops with their protruding miradors[1] of dark wooden latticed screens in the upper floor. This street led down to the Plaza de Armas de Lima, that wide open park decorated with palms, which was the traditional centre of the city.

He crossed the street to enter the plaza, found a bench seat, and sat down. The rays of the setting sun gave the twin spires of the Cathedral on the other side of the plaza a rosy glow. It was the time when families gathered in their homes after their daily toil, although a few old men sat together on one of the benches eagerly discussing the affairs of the day which only they could solve. Soon the lanterns would be lit and eventually the good people of Lima would come out for a walk in the cool evening air.

---

[1] A lookout – here as long bay windows covered with ornate wooden fretwork.

An old lady was selling empanadas[2] from her small heated metal trolly a few paces down from where he was sitting, he suddenly realised that he was hungry. He purchased two for a few centimos and returned to his bench, savouring the rich aroma of their contents and their delightful crusty pastry. He quenched his thirst from a public drinking fountain. This was part of the large bronze fountain, with its surmounted angel playing the trumpet known as the Angel of Fame, which stood in the centre of the plaza. He looked up at the angel with its trumpet and wondered with despair how he would ever find fame now that he had left his family and regiment.

He wandered out of the plaza, past the beautiful cathedral with its three huge doors

---

[2] An empanada is a baked or fried turnover consisting of pastry and filling which may consist of meat, cheese, tomato, corn, olives or other ingredients. The name comes from the Galician verb translated as "enbreaded", that is, wrapped or coated in bread.

into a side street. Perhaps it was Providence or simply the randomness of his wandering but after a few minutes walking, he found himself outside of a coaching inn. Its large double doors were open, inside the lanterns were bright as the ostlers and coachmen were pushing a large coach into one of the several bays in the outer courtyard.

A cold darkness had now fallen upon the city and Xavier felt the need for sleep. The large sign on the wall to one side of the open archway read 'Pachakamaq Posada y Carruaje Empresa'[3] and in fine print 'Todas las rutas del Norte'[4]. The bright lanterns and the need for rest led him into the small office which had an open door in the side of the archway. Here he found a rotund, florid man

---

[3] 'Pachakamaq Inn and Coach Company' – Pachakamaq is the Quechua name for an archaeological site well north of Lima. The ancient people here worshiped the creator god Pacha Kamaq.
[4] 'All routes North'

examining his books of daily accounts. He looked up as Xavier entered.

"Ah, buenas noches señor"[5] he said with a smile." How can I be of service?"

Xavier put down his bag and said with some apprehension "Do you have a room for the night?"

"Certainly! For a gentleman such as yourself, there is always a room!" he replied genially reaching for a key, one of many which hung on a board on the wall behind the counter.

"Is there a coach going north soon?" Xavier asked.

"You are in luck, señor. There is one leaving for Trujillo at eight tomorrow morning with connecting coaches which go even further.

---

[5] Literally 'Good night, sir' but on greeting would be 'good evening'.

Would you like to buy a ticket? It is very quiet for this time of year."

"Yes, how far north do your coaches go?" Xavier asked with no particular destination in mind.

The innkeeper looked around as though there were a crowd of people nearby and he wished to keep a secret. He gave a smile and winked his eye.

"We can go all the way to Zarumilla on the border with Ecuador if you wish..." he said in a conspiratorial manner "... and even across it if our friends are manning the border. Do you have the necessary papers?"

Xavier felt perplexed. He had not thought much past simply leaving Lima and forgetting the painful meeting with his father.

"I have my Identity Papers…. what else would I need, señor?"

Another leering wink from the innkeeper.

"No problem. Just a border pass is all that is needed. Now that we have the new telegraph here in Lima, I would send your details to our agent in Machala in Ecuador and he will arrange for you to pick up the pass at Zarumilla. Of course, there would be a small charge for this service, you understand?"

Xavier was well aware of such border transactions, having crossed several in his days as a young officer. Little would be required but his personal details and a good reason for travelling. He took out his Identification Papers and printed his real name in the register on the desk and gave the title of 'traveller' for his reason to enter Ecuador.

The innkeeper took his papers and studied them with some care then returned them with the key to the room.

"They seem all in order, Señor Aguirre. Your room is number six upstairs. I will see that all is arranged should you have to cross the border."

Xavier paid the required amount for his room, the coach to Trujillo and the 'extra service' entered in the receipt then took the key. Thanking the innkeeper for his help, he picked up his bag and climbed the stairs to the upper balcony to his room for the emotional rest he solely needed.

The next morning, Xavier woke feeling refreshed for the first time in days. He dressed, repacked his small bag and went downstairs to a light breakfast of coffee and sweet bread rolls. Promptly at eight, the coach driver announced that all was ready then Xavier climbed into the coach and put his bag up on the small rack above his head. The innkeeper's comment about the lack of business was not wrong and Xavier found himself to be the only occupant as the coach trundled out of the archway and down the cobbled streets of Lima.

The main highway closely followed the coast along the narrow strip of land which separated the foothills of the Andes Mountains to the east from the Pacific Ocean to the west.

Most of this part of Peru is desert. This is due to the rain shadow effect of the Andes stopping the moisture-laden winds from the east, and the cold Humboldt Current which flows northwards parallel to the coast and so does not provide much moisture inland. Water in abundance only existed where the many small rivers, running down their narrow valleys, took the waters from the snows of the Andes and cast them into the sea. Near the end of these valleys, small settlements had developed and crops were able to be grown to supplement the rich fishing which was to be had in the cold, upwelling waters rich in nutrients along the coast.

Now well out of the city, Xavier looked out of the window of the coach through the heavy veil of the Garúa, that sea mist which regularly blows in across the cold waters of the Humboldt Current. It would be a fine day later on, he thought as he pulled his travelling cloak tighter around his shoulders, but for now, the air inside the coach felt cool and moist.

The trip to Huarmey, where the coach would stop for the night, was uneventful as Xavier was alone in the coach as it travelled northwards along the coastal road. Only the view from the windows offered some respite from the boredom and the rough motion of the coach. Eventually the sea mist cleared giving him an occasional and expansive view of the Pacific Ocean now sparkling blue in the morning sunlight. For the most part, the inland view was of a flat dry desert, only broken by the few small patches of green vegetation, scanty crops and small adobe settlements where some small coastal stream came down from the unseen mountains well to the east.

After what seemed to be an eternity, the coach pulled into a small inn in the village of Huacho. This was simply a larger village than the many small settlements through which they had passed. It occupied a large patch of green around the mouth of the Rio Huaura around which could be seen crops of rice, cotton, sugarcane and different grains. It was only a short stop so that the horses could be changed and a few locals clambered up onto the seats on top of the coach. Xavier went into the inn and had some refreshment before returning to his seat. Then suddenly, with new drivers, the coach rattled forward for the last leg of the journey.

More flat desert lands with the occasional bare light brown sandy hill rolled past until the country opened up into extensive green fields with some trees as they approached the village of Barranca near the mouth of the Río Pativilca. Thereafter, the landscape slipped once again back into the dry coastal desert with its weird conical hills until night fell and the coach finally pulled to its night stop in the small settlement of Huarmey.

The village of Huarmey was small. It consisted of mainly single-story adobe houses with a few open-front shops on the main road. The coaching inn, the Posada de la Sagrada Familia, was one of the few houses which had two stories. There was no inner courtyard as with some of the more traditional posadas in the city, but there was a walled yard on one side which the coach entered though a wide gate. Inside, the rooms were clean and the beds soft.

Breakfast the next morning consisted of pastries and coffee with banana fritters. The weather in the early morning promised to be fine once the sea mist had cleared. Promptly at eight, the coach and horses were brought out of the yard and Xavier boarded for the last leg of the journey to Trujillo, some 240 kilometres to the north. It would be another long day through the coastal desert, only to be broken by a short change of horses and lunch at Chimbote on the Rio Santa, one of the few green oases along this part of the coast. As before, there were no other passengers inside the coach, but several of the locals with their baskets and sacks climbed up onto the seats above.

The dusty road between Huarmey and Chimbote offered no respite from the agitated motions of the coach nor the monotonous vista of the brown, pebbly hills and the seeming endless flat plains beyond. It was well after dark when the coach finally entered the lively brightness of the city of Trujillo.

The coaching stop here was also just a walled yard with a small but neat-looking office in one corner closest to the gate. The manager was welcoming, gregarious and quickly arranged for Xavier's ticket to Zarumilla on the border with Ecuador. He lamented that it would be another four days journey away and tomorrow being a Sunday, there would not be another coach until the day after. Xavier was tired and despite the attraction of such a big city, he was glad of the manager's recommendation of a good hotel just a few paces up the street. He was not surprized when the manager proudly informed him that the hotel belonged to his cousin, Rodrigo.

The Hotel de Los Angeles was unpretentious and it was the owner himself who saw to Xavier's need for a quiet room for some rest after a hard day's travel across the heat, dust and monotony of the coastal desert. His room was near the back on the hotel's second and highest floor, it was large, well-furnished and clean.

He placed his small bag onto the top of the dresser near its blue and white porcelain water basin and jug, stripped off his outer clothing, extinguished the small candle by the bedside and threw himself onto the bed. He was desperately tired after the long day but his mind was troubled. All of the words of his father's rejection came back in the dark silence to trouble him.

Sleep eluded him so he sat up and lit the candle. On the small bedside table near the lamp was a small, black-covered Bible. He picked it up and opened it at random. It was the Book of Exodus from which he read. He read of the Israelites wandering in the desert looking for their promised land and he could not help but think that this is what he was doing also. But there was no Moses here to lead him in his journey, nor was there a promised land at its end. He put down the Bible and eventually drifted into a fitful sleep awaking at sunrise feeling tired and jaded.

The next morning being a Sunday, Xavier dressed in his second set of clothing, had a light breakfast and went out into the street. He decided to walk the two blocks to the cathedral in the Plaza de Armes and go to mass. It was not that he was a particularly religious man, it was just a matter of habit. He had been taken to mass every Sunday morning by his mother and also when he went to Military School and then at the Academy, Sunday Mass was always compulsory affair; even as an officer in the cavalry, there was always Church Parade even when the unit was in the field.

Xavier walked down the cobble street with its narrow pedestrian path and continuation of walls and two-story buildings with their grated windows and heavy doors. For the most part they were unpainted with just the bare plaster, sometimes crazed and flaking, showing. A few of the better houses were painted in bright colours and the gratings at the windows and the upper balconies were painted in white or blue.

There was the usual number of people on the road at this early hour for a Sunday; some in their best clothes heading towards the cathedral as was he, and other pushing small carts or carrying bundles oblivious to the sanctity of the day. He arrived at the next cross street and looked up at the street signs on the bare wall of the corner building; 'Jirón Independencia[6]' the sign read. But of course! He remembered now his history from his early schooldays. Trujillo had proclaimed its independence from its Spanish masters on the twenty-ninth of December in 1820; seven months before the proclamation of the independence in the rest of the country. This was ironic, he thought, as the city was founded by the Conquistador Diego de Almagro in 1534, calling it *Trujillo* after the home city of Francisco Pizarro, the Spaniard responsible for the conquest and subjugation of Peru.

Xavier crossed the spacious plaza with its wide pathways leading in as spokes in a wheel to a central area fringed with small gardens and palm trees. The cathedral, as was usually the custom in many south American cities, was opposite the

---

[6] 'Independence Street'

government buildings across the plaza. It was in the Baroque style and unusually was situated only on one corner and not occupying a central position. It was beautifully painted in a dark yellow with attractive white trim, framed by two short bell towers.

Inside the Cathedral Basilica of St. Mary, Xavier was initially struck by the feeling of openness; this was no sombre house of a cheerless God but one of light and beauty. A place where God would speak with laugher and joy not with sadness on the follies of his children. To be sure, he found the altar pieces, which adorned the front and sides of the building, to be beautifully ornate wood carvings featuring the Holy Family and many of the saints, but it was the ceiling which made the most impact on his senses. The walls were in brilliant white plaster with columns and archways painted in a bright yellow but the roof was decorated in many frescos painted with pastel colours. The ceiling consisted of several separate arches and the paintings on their interiors depicted a variety of colourful images of the lives of the saints. Xavier was enthralled by the lightness and beauty of the cathedral's interior. It was this colourful interior, rather than the Mass itself which lifted his spirits. After mass, he left the cathedral, stopping only to place a few coins in the hand of the old peasant lady who sat at the door, before he walked back to his hotel.

The next morning, Xavier packed his few belongings ready to walk back down to the coaching station. Here was the usual bustle of loading goods and preparing the coach and horses. The coach was ready to go on its long journey north to Zarumilla and Xavier was delighted to find that, on this leg of the journey at least, he was to have some company.

There was only one other passenger in the cabin of the coach; the seats and roof above were of course, occupied by many locals with their many bags of belongings and goods to sell.

As the coach rattled out of the gates of the coaching station, Xavier's fellow traveller looked across at him and said:
"Buenos días señor. It looks like we are going to be going to be together for a while. Permit me to introduce myself as Dr. Eduardo Chávez – for my sins I am Head of Antiquities at the Museum of Natural History and Antiquities at Lima," he said.

He was an elderly man, probably in his fifties, Xavier thought, inclined to be over-weight but with a round and smiling face.

"Mucho Gusto[7], Dr. Chávez." Xavier replied with a slight nod of his head. "Permit me to name myself as Xavier Aguirre, from Lima."

It would be a welcome relief to now have some company on his journey, and the old man seemed to be a friendly type. "You seemed to be going in the wrong direction." Xavier said with a smile.

"Ah, ah!" laughed the old man. "Sometimes we academics get a little lost in our bearings, that is true, but no, this time I am on the right track. You see, I am going to Guayaquil to catch a steamer for San Francisco. I am delivering a scientific paper there. And you, señor?" he replied.

"Oh, nothing so important, Dr. Chávez, I am simply a man looking to explore Ecuador for my own education," Xavier said, trying to

---

[7] "Pleased to meet you."

find some reason for his flight from his homeland.

The coach now rattled out of the main centre of Trujillo and into the dusty road which led further north. They were once more travelling across the flat, dry desert which led from the sea to the hills further east. It would be another long day of travelling.

Out of curiosity and perhaps to relieve to inevitable boredom, Xavier leaned back in his seat and asked the old man what his intended scientific paper was about.

With this, the old man became very animated and excited. "Ah, a very interesting topic and it is a most important one for our country. You see I am an Antiquarian – or perhaps I should use the modern term of Archaeologist. Would you like to hear of my work?"

"Yes indeed!" Xavier replied with some enthusiasm. Archaeology was not a topic which featured in his military education, but his heritage on his mother's side of the family gave him an interest in the lives of the people who lived in Peru in past times.

"Well, now. Where shall I start? There is much history to be learnt – and just only a few kilometres from where we are now, you understand?" he replied pointing with his hand out of the coach window and to the desert beyond.

The old man leant back in his seat and closed his eyes as if to help his memory of a subject which he knew well and was dear to his heart. "I was a student and then a colleague of our great savant, Mariano Eduardo de Rivero y Ustariz. Have you heard of him, Señor Aguirre?" the old man said, opening his eyes.

"Alas, no." Xavier replied "Regretfully, I know little of archaeology."

"Ah well, you perhaps will one day, if your studies lean towards the sciences. He was one of Peru's greatest man of learning; a student of geology, mineralogy, chemistry and of course, archaeology. He was also a politician and a diplomat but alas, he has been dead now for some time. A great loss to our country." The old man pulled out a small handkerchief from his belt and dried his eyes.

"The dust is becoming a little troublesome." Xavier replied with some compassion.

"Thank you, señor." The old man said. "Perhaps you would like to hear about our work?"

"Yes, I would like to hear about your work, Dr. Chávez. I know little about this part of the country and less of its people. Besides, we have a long journey ahead of us and your work then would be of great interest to me." Xavier replied.

The old man sat up and looked out of the window of the coach beyond to the dusty plain which separated the highway from the sea. He pointed out of the window towards the low, brown hills between the road and the sea:

"Out there, not five kilometres from the centre of Trujillo in the desert of the Moche Valley lies another city; the city of Chan Chan. My teacher, Mariano de Rivero had been working with the famed Swiss Antiquarian, Jakob von Tschudi on the site of this city attempting to discover how its people, the Chimú, lived. Regretfully my teacher died a few years ago and Herr von Tschudi went to continue his work in Brazil.

I and a few of the younger students continued our work in Chan Chan."

The coach rattled along the dusty road and the old man continued his story:

"Chan Chan must have been a wonderful city. It is still a great wonder today when you think of how the Chimú were able to live here in such a dry land. They had the rivers of course, which we now call the Rio Chicama and the Río Moche, they also had the sea for fishing, but it still must have been an hostile environment. We will be crossing the Río Chicama soon, by the way.

In their language, 'Chan' means 'sun', so their city's double name could be best translated as 'Great Sun'. Which is surprising as unlike the Incas who conquered them, their main deity was 'Shi' the Moon."

"How old was their city?" Xavier enquired.

The old man looked out of the window at the dry lands west of the road and then turned to look at his companion.

"We think that the Chimú developed from an earlier people, the Moche who had been here from about 900 A.D., but their empire really did not begin to expand until about two hundred years later. The Chimor empire extended north along the coast into Ecuador and well south of here along the coastline of northern Peru. Unfortunately, they became a subject people under the Inca after 1470 when the Incan emperor Topa Inca Yupanqui offered them inclusion or destruction. It was only another fifty years or so before the arrival of the Spanish which then meant the total destruction of both empires."

"I have seen many Incan buildings near my home in Cuzco. Were those of the Chimú as mighty as those?" Xavier asked.

"It would be difficult to make such a comparison, my friend." The old man said with a smile. "You see Chan Chan was built entirely of adobe – mud bricks – out of the desert soil whereas the Inca had the stone of their high mountains. To be sure, some say that Chan Chan was greater because they did build here in the desert. Their city covered almost twenty square kilometres with extensive highly decorated walls. It also had a dense urban centre containing several large and extravagant architectural zones called *Ciudadelas* which each housed plazas, storerooms, and burial platforms for the royal classes. The lower classes of this hierarchical society lived in a series of smaller, joined rooms. They were more likely artisans and merchants with many of the population also engaged in agriculture and fishing.

The Chimú were brilliant craftsmen in fine metal working of copper, gold, silver, and bronze but they are best known for their distinctive black and dark brown shiny pottery. This was often fashioned in the shape of an animal or a human figure sitting or standing on a bottle with six flat faces.

They were also outstanding engineers and built many canals to carry water to their fields. There is even evidence that they had started a grand canal to divert water from the Río Chicama through twenty kilometres of desert to Chan Chan, but this project was never completed.

The Moche civilisation from which the Chimú developed also were noted for their building. Just south of modern Trujillo for example, they built two huge temples or *huacas*, the Huaca del Sol and the Huaca de la Luna - the Temples of the Sun and the Moon.

The Huaca del Sol was built with adobe bricks on many extensive and high stepped levels, but now, much has collapsed and eroded away. Now the great temple only resembles an enormous mound of clay.

The Huaca de la Luna is much smaller, having fewer levels, but then the Moche had the habit of building new temples over the old with the passing of each priestly dynasty, so that each of them probably represented a different place of worship. By burying them so, the Moche preserved the inner temples with their paintings and friezes from the ravages of time and conquest. Today, they are often called 'pyramids' and compared to those of Central America, but this may not be a fair comparison as they were probably more complex in their shape.

Truly great feats of engineering, but now these temples and the great city of Chan Chan have crumbled into the desert from whence they came; and of course, the Spanish have looted as much as they could when they arrived. But – "the old man sighed and again looked out across the desert – "who knows what future archaeologists will find below those mounds of dust?"

Xavier found the old professor's talk about the ancient civilizations of northern Peru fascinating. He was, of course, proud of his own ancestry which came from the heartland of the Incan Empire which had absorbed Chan Chan and many of the other earlier tribal groups in this western part of the continent. He knew that with the Incan expansion in the fifteenth century, most tribes had been prepared to accept the Incan terms of joining their well-ordered society or perishing. They were brutal times, but the Incan Empire was a benevolent society to those who wished to retain their tribal identities but would accept the rules and benefits of being part of the Incan Empire.

Xavier was also interested in the way that the old man spoke. His story of the Moche and the Chimú was not some boring lecture by a tired academic but a stirring tale of real and ingenious people who lived here in the desert and flourished against great hardships in such a hostile environment.

Capítulo Tres:
Cuentos de Monjas y Espíritus
(Chapter Three: Tales of Nuns and Spirits)

The coach rattled on over the dusty road; the acrid smell of the desert permeated every part of their small, confined world which lurched this way and that with every rut in the road. Xavier felt some compassion for those people who rode on the roof of the coach. They would be feeling the coach's motion more than those below but they were hardy people, those of the western desert who bore their discomfort with the usual stoicism; suffering was part of their daily lives and was accepted with good humour.

Eventually the coach stopped briefly at a small coaching inn on the outskirts of the small city of Chiclayo for refreshments and a change of horses and drivers. As Xavier and Dr. Chávez climbed out of the carriage, the old man moved his arm around as if to encompass the entire vista and said:

"Welcome to Santa María de los Valles de Chiclayo, Señor Aguirre, a great outpost of the Moche culture!"

Xavier looked around and saw the usual flat, dusty desert to the southwest but to the east there was a line of steep hills and cliffs rising out of the desert on the far horizon. They had crossed a stream which the old man had called the Río Chancay but which the locals call the Reque when it trickles into the Pacific a few kilometres to the east. Now there was an abundance of green grass and crops and some small, wiry trees. The old man touched Xavier's sleeve and said, almost in a conspiratorial voice that the in the Mochican language the name of this city probably came from *Chiclayap* which means 'place where there are green branches'.

Their stay was not long but they were well-received by the owner of the inn who introduced himself as Señor Pérez; a happy rotund man, with a permanent smile stretched across his broad, brown face. As they sat beneath a small grove of Cinchona trees which had been planted next to the inn, the old man reached across and pulled off a small piece of the bark of one of the trees.

"Do you know what this is, Señor Aguirre?" he said with a wry smile.

Botany had never been part of Xavier's education, so he looked up into the face of the smiling academic and confessed his ignorance.

"Why, Señor Aguirre, this is one of the saving plants of the Human race! It is the bark of this tree, the Cinchona, a member of the genus of flowering plants in the family *Rubiaceae* and apart from giving us the excellent remedy against malaria, quinine, its other relative also gives us coffee. It is said that the name of this tree comes from that of Luis Jerónimo de Cabrera, who was the fourth Count of Chinchón and Viceroy of Peru, whose wife was cured of the fever after taking this local remedy. The tribes here abouts and elsewhere in Peru have been using this bark crushed in a little water for a cure against the fever for ages. And shame on you!" the old man said with a gentle chide to his companion." As a good Peruvian, did you not recognise the very tree that is on our coat of arms!

Xavier did feel some shame. Not so much as not recognising the 'fever tree' of the Jesuits, but at have an ignorance of its patriotic significance and his own lack of knowledge.

They continued on the next leg of their journey; and it was a long one so that they did not see the welcoming lights of the city of Piura until well into the night. By this time, both the old man and Xavier were too tired to care for any socialisation so after a short meal of seco de carne[1] they both retired to their rooms. Tomorrow would be another long day.

The next morning, as the rays of the sun just edged their way over the dark peaks on the eastern horizon, Xavier went down to breakfast seeking out his new companion, Dr. Chávez, about a question which had been bothering him all night.

He found the old man sitting on a bench in front of the inn and smoking his pipe. As Xavier approached, he took out his pipe and pointed to the coach which was already being loaded for the next long leg to the Ecuadorian border.

---

[1] A beef stew using local beef in a fermented corn beverage, *chicha de jora,* and cilantro (coriander) and often served with beans and rice.

"It seems that we are to have some civilised company on our journey, today." He said with a smile.

Xavier looked up towards the coach and noticed two nuns standing at the end of the coach; the eldest one carefully watching the loading of their possessions onto the roof of the coach.

Xavier had had little to do with nuns and so thought very little of the old man's comments. Perhaps it would be a pleasant journey, perhaps not. He had never known nuns to be outgoing and talkative. He had forgotten the question which he was going to ask his learned companion; it could wait until later he thought.

The carriage being loaded, Xavier and Chávez waited respectfully as the two nuns climbed up into the carriage and took their seats facing in the direction that the carriage would travel. Xavier ushered the older man in first and he took the window seat directly opposite the elder nun. He gave he a half-smile and a nod of his head as he sat down. Xavier followed and sat next to him opposite the younger nun, giving a faint smile to no one in particular.

"¡Vamos![2]" cried the driver and they were off on the last leg before the Ecuadorian border. The old man leaned across and said to the older nun:

"Permit me to introduce us; your new travelling companions. I am Dr. Eduardo Chávez – for my sins I am Head of Antiquities at the Museum of Natural History and Antiquities at Lima and this is my new friend, Señor Xavier Aguirre del Rio, also from Lima."

---

[2] "Let's go!"

His introduction over, the old man sat back in the seat with a satisfied smile. For a short time, there was silence. Then the older nun, feeling that a reply was warranted said without moving from her seat and with her facial expression unchanging replied in heavily accented Spanish:

"Buenos días señores.[3] I am Sister Geraldine Dillon and this my Novice, Sister Valeria. We are Sisters of Mercy from our Mission near Iquitos."

The young nun looked up for a brief moment and gave a weak smile then lowered her head once more.

"That is a long way from Piura, Reverend Mother!" the old man said in English with a smile ... and just as wet as your home country, if I hear the accent correctly."

---

[3] "Good morning, sirs."

Sister Geraldine gave the old man a stern look of disapproval and then sat back and laughed:

"But at least the rain is warmer in Iquitos, and besides I am Irish! Dr. Chávez but English unfortunately is the language of my parents – God rest them!"

"Ah! My apologies, Reverend Mother. We Latinos sometimes find such differences confusing" apologised the old man with a depreciating wave of his hand. "You do not find the climate in the jungle rather difficult?" he continued.

"To be sure, señor." Sister Geraldine replied and then with the faintest of smiles said: "But we Sisters of Mercy are a hardy lot!"

The old man laughed at this comment and added:

"Still, it must be hard for you in that 'green hell' sometimes."

The formality of the first meeting now somewhat broken, Sister Geraldine continued:

"We endure it for the sake of our people but alas, Sister Valeria contracted malaria and so I am taking her to Zorritos. There at the Iglesia Señor de los Milagros[4] she will help Father Ignacio with his Parish school and hopefully regain her health."

"Ah, back in Piura there was a small grove of Cinchona trees; perhaps the local apothecary in the next village could prescribe some extract of the quinine for the good sister?" The old man replied with some sympathy.

---

[4] Iglesia Señor de los Milagros – 'the Church of the Lord of Miracles'

"Thank you, señor," Sister Geraldine replied "we have that same medication given to us by our parishioners. They call the sickness *karkametstace*[5] and treat it with the same plant which they call *quina-quina,* which means 'holy bark' in the Quechua language of the Inca."

Xavier had been quiet up until now; happy to have the gregarious old man lead the conversation, but he now was interested in what Sister Geraldine had to say. His grandmother had taught him to speak her native tongue of Aymara and also the more widely spoken Quechua language. She had also told him about many of the ancient customs and uses of local plants, minerals and animals.

---

[5] In the language of the Asháninka [ah-SHAH-nin-kah,] people who live along the Marañón River, one of the headwaters of the Amazon in north-eastern Peru. They were known by the Incas as *Anti* or *Campa.*

"Do you use many of the local remedies, Reverend Mother? I am most interested to hear about such things." Xavier asked with some enthusiasm.

"Why yes, Señor Aguirre. Our Father Matías is of the Society of Jesus and has been at the Mission for many years. He is a very old man whom our parishioners love greatly. He has accepted their ways and teaches them gently rather than forcing the Lord's word upon them. Our sisters also do what we can to heal the sick and, in this regard, we have had considerable help from the local brujo – what we in English would call a 'witchdoctor'. He sometimes scares us by suddenly arriving in our midst all covered in paint and feathers but he really is a friendly old man and he and Father Matías are good friends. Mind you! – the locals are also scared of his powers and sometimes call him the *Chullachaqui*[6] behind

---

[6] [Coola-KHAR–tee] Spanish form of the Quechua word for a malignant jungle spirit. Ohers say that it is the embodiment of the jungle itself which pervades every living thing.

his back. They say that he is really the spirit of the jungle itself, but even as a good Christian, I am still Irish and so I do not contradict them. Still, he is good to us and has many cures for our jungle ailments, even if they involve some revolting rituals and mumbo jumbo," she laughed.

Xavier now sat on the edge of his seat. He had heard about such brujos from his grandmother – every people seem to have their wise men and women who used folk medicines mixed with superstition and ritual. His education had been a classical one and later had been concerned with military history, affairs and tactics. The stories which his grandmother had told him in happier times at home when he was a boy had always been of great interest but had largely been put aside as he grew into manhood.

"Please, Reverend Mother, can you tell us about some of these cures and your work in the jungle?" he asked. "I am sure that Dr. Chávez, being a natural philosopher would also be interested."

"Indeed, I would," spoke the old man. "We Antiquarians tend to become too occupied with our old ruins – me being one of them – to learn about such things," he laughed.

Sister Geraldine sat back in her seat and looked down at Sister Valeria who had now fallen asleep and had rested her head against the side of the carriage.

"Ah! Poor child. The malaria makes her tired and she has had a long journey." she said, then looking more directly at the two men continued: "Well now! It is indeed an interesting thing to live in the jungle. To be sure it is! As I have said, it has been a long journey for us poor souls but if you would like to hear a little of it then perhaps our present journey will not take as long."

"It would have taken you both a long time to come from your Mission, Reverend Mother?" the old man asked.

"Yes, señor." She replied earnestly. "Iquitos can only be reached by river and even the settlements with roads to the outside world are themselves remote. We had to walk for two days before we got to the city and then come by canoe up the Rio Marañón until it meets its tributary, the Rio Huallaga. Beyond that, the Río Marañón becomes difficult to negotiate and has many pongos[7] to get through. Even in the lower stretches, the water in both of these rivers still moved fast and we were paddling upstream for several weeks until we reached the city of Yurimaguas. Our boys were strong paddlers, as they do this trip often, and there were many settlements and plantations along the

---

[7] The word 'pongo' is a corruption of the Quechua word *punku* meaning a gateway and is a type of canyon or narrow gorge along rivers in Peru, especially on the Marañón River.

rivers for our overnight stays, but it was still an exhausting trip up river.[8]"

"You had no problems with hostile tribes?" Xavier asked.

"No, Señor Aguirre. I believe that our friend, the Brujo Juan had spread the word through the jungle that we were under his protection. They still hunt for heads there you know and two women would be easy prey."

"Please go on, Reverend Mother." The old man asked.

"Well, señores. The river journey was only the beginning. Yurimaguas is a lovely city – founded by the Jesuits, I believe in 1710 – but it is still at the end of a long road. The coast

---

[8] Come with the author on a trip down the Rio Madre de Dios, another headwater of the Amazon south of the Marañón and trek into the jungle looking for Spider Monkeys at: https://www.youtube.com/watch?v=VhJ7Ve1FbL0

is still about six hundred miles to the west and that journey also took us several weeks and through the cities of Tarapoto, and Jaén de Bracamoros – the Apostolic Vicariate of St. Francis Xavier.

"You have had a long journey, Sister Geraldine and through such inhospitable country," Xavier said with some compassion, but tell me more about the jungle. You see, my people are from the mountains and know very little about the jungles to our east."

"Yes, Sister. Please do!" interjected the old man. "You see, I am an Antiquarian and have a great interest in different cultures. Who is this 'Chullachaqui' whom you mentioned earlier?" he asked. "I know of many of the gods of the coastal and mountain peoples, but I have never heard that name before."

Sister Geraldine looked out of the window of the coach to the distant mountains across the flat desert and thought for a moment. Then she gave a smile and clasped her hands together on her lap.

"Well, now señores, Chullachaqui is the very spirit of the jungle; one to be feared, especially if you do the jungle harm like clearing its forests or unnecessarily killing its animals. The peoples of the jungle, especially the Asháninka who live along the Marañón River, would never harm the trees nor animals except for their own basic needs and it said that Chullachaqui tolerates this, but they are still scared of him. I have only lived in the jungle for the last five years but even from the beginning, I could feel the spirit of the jungle. Father Mateo has lived there for a long time and he respects and has accepted many of the local's beliefs."

"Why do the natives fear this Chullachaqui?" asked the old man.

Sister Geraldine looked up into his face and smiled. "It is said that he is an ugly old man short in statue and having one different foot and that he can change his shape to any animal in the forest. In fact, his name comes from the Quechua *'ch'ulla chaqui'* which means 'different foot' as one of them is apparently like a hoof. It is said that if he is angered, he will change his shape to that of a loved one of the people who had caused offence and then lures them into the deep jungle. Once they have followed him, they find that he has suddenly disappeared and left them lost in the jungle to die. Even the most expert of jungle trackers would find their way out."

"He is like the Kelpie of your Irish legends, then Sister?" the old man said with a smile.

"Oh no, to be sure!" the nun replied with some shock. "Our kelpie is a water creature who eats children! We call such creatures the 'Na Púcaí' and whilst they can change their shape – usually to a beautiful woman or a lovely horse – to lure children or fishermen to drown in the water, they are not like the Chullachaqui. Our friend the Brujo Juan will tell you that the Chullachaqui is the protector of all life in the forest and is generally disinterested in the activities of human folk – unless they interfere with the life of the forest."

The coach rattled on along on the narrow road through the dusty desert and Sister Geraldine told of the many myths which she had heard from Father Matías during the countless hot, rainy days and lonely nights at their Mission. He had heard them directly from the Brujo Juan and so they must be true and Xavier and the old man were captivated by these stories. She told them about

Yacumama, the 'mother of the water,' and the protective spirit of the Amazon River itself. It is a gigantic anaconda that almost always appears when it rains and she told them about Tunche, the evil spirit of the forest. He is the ghost of a man tormented by evil and whose soul wanders in the dark making a sharp whistling sound which announces the death of the listener much like the Banshee, the female spirit in Irish folklore who wailing and shrieking in the night is meant to herald the death of a family member.

The stories were a welcome respite from their arduous journey and soon they saw the brilliant blue of the Pacific Ocean as the road had turned westward and came out onto the coast at the town of Talara. Here they changed horses and drivers and were able to rest while having a small meal. Sisters Geraldine and Valeria took their leave to attend to their ablutions whilst Xavier and the old academic found a bench under a shady tree which looked out over the water.

As it was only a short stop, soon the coach was on its way again. Some of the passengers on the roof had alighted at Talara and others had taken their place. From here, the road briefly returned eastward back into the desert and then abruptly north until it again reached the sea near the town of Organos. From here, the road was never far from the sea and the fresh sea air gave some comfort from the dry dust of the inland waste. Eventually, near nightfall, the coach arrived at Zorritos but continued on through the town directly to the Iglesia Señor de los Milagros which was a few kilometres north of the centre of town on the main road.

Reluctantly, Xavier and his companion said farewell to the two nuns as the coach stopped near the gate of the church where there was group of local people giving them a joyful welcome; all bearing flowers and bright smiles.

It was only about twenty kilometres from Zorritos to their final destination at Zarumilla. Night had fallen but it was clear from the lights of the coach and from the many small farm houses, that the desert had finally surrendered to a climate which was less harsh, supporting many crops, including tall rows of corn, lining the road leading into the town.

The coaching stop here was at a well-presented posada. The coach rattled on the cobbles as it went through the high archway leading into the spacious central courtyard. The passengers on the roof quickly gathered up their small bundles and headed off into the night whilst Xavier followed Dr. Chávez into the small office which opened out onto one of the walls of the broad archway. Here they were greeted by the proprietor, Señor

Lopez and his wife. Both had that well-fed and happy countenance that seemed to be a common feature of inn-keepers who were doing well and now meeting new customers.

Xavier wrote his name into the book which was provided for such events and Señora Lopez read it and said with a smile:

"Ah, Señor Aguirre, welcome to Zarumilla. We have a package for you from my cousin in Machala in Ecuador as arranged."

Xavier took the bundle of papers which were neatly enclosed in an unmarked brown envelope and discretely asked about what gratuity he should offer. The price was agreeable and he soon joined his travelling companion in the small lounge which was in an adjoining room. A small supper was served by a charming young lady who from her youth and appearance was most likely

Señorita Lopez; country posadas were often family affairs he thought.

The posada was on the northern outskirts of the city so it was only about a kilometre to the border at Aguas Verdes or 'Green Waters' where the bridge goes over the Río Zarumilla and into the bustling town of Huaquillas in Ecuador. After a good breakfast, he took his old companion by the arm and said:

"Well, my good doctor. It is time for a short stroll as our coach is now waiting on the other side of the customs office across the border."

This was a common way of crossing borders in South America and both men were used to such a short walk from one country into another. Unlike many border crossings which tend to be austere and full of dread as to whether or not one's papers were in order; the crossing here more resembled a market on a fiesta day. The streets were full of people and there were many street stalls under shady, multi-coloured umbrellas. They passed under a large, red sign which read 'Gracias por su visita[9]' with the coat of arms of Peru embellished above and further down the street was another high road sign, blue in colour, which read 'Bienvenidos a Ecuador[10]'. We still had another day of coach travel until we reach the port of Guayaquil.

---

[9] 'Thanks for your visit'
[10] 'Welcome to Ecuador'

Capítulo Cuatro:
En la Tierra Prometida
(Chapter Four: Into the Promised Land)

It was nightfall before the coach stopped at the posada in the village of Durán, just across the Río Guayas from the rest of Guayaquil, the main port of Ecuador. Our journey had been long and not as entertaining as previous trips, mostly due to the presence of a fat merchant, Señor Gordón and his equally rotund wife. They made it quite clear upon entering the carriage that amicable conversation was inappropriate and spent much of the day loudly sleeping. Xavier and his old friend spoke softly of various things which they had seen or heard of in their different lives or remarking on the countryside which was now hilly and lush with vegetation, including stands of tall trees; very different to the monotonous landscape which they had seen for the past few days.

At the night stop at Durán, Xavier and the old academic had one last meal to celebrate the good doctor's arrival at the port and Xavier wished him a peaceful sea voyage to his conference in San Francisco. For Xavier, his exodus from Lima was beginning to become tiring. He liked travel, but the daily routine of coach travel with overnight stops in small hotels or posadas was beginning to take its toll on his humour. After the meal, he said goodnight to his friend, and again wishing him a safe journey, retired to his small room.

The next morning, Xavier again met his old friend at the door of the Posada where the old man was loading his valise onto a small trap. This would take him the short distance to the steamer dock not far away at Malecón on this side of the river. Xavier had been pleased to find that a connecting coach to Quito, more than two hundred kilometres away up in the mountains, would be departing in a short time from a coaching station just a few hundred metres away.

With a final farewell to his friend, Xavier took his bag and walked off down the main road to the coaching station. Here, after a short wait he was able to board, along with several talkative students who were also going to the capital.

The journey this time was much more pleasant. The students were excited about returning to their university in Quito. They spoke freely to Xavier about their studies and aspirations for the future. He enjoyed these small conversations as they reminded him of his youth and his days at the Military Academy. The vista from the coach windows was also a pleasant surprise as it reminded him of similar countryside on the slopes of the Andes east of his birthplace, Lima.

The road headed east to Milagro then turned abruptly north at Cumanda then followed the mountain range, gradually climbing up its slopes to Ambato where the coach stopped briefly for a change of horses and drivers as well as a rest for the passengers. From here, the road followed the high plain with an occasional view of tall, snow-capped mountains including the magnificent cone of the Volcán Cotopaxi well to the east. Eventually, well after darkness had fallen, the lights of the southern outskirts of Quito came into view.

The coachman had recommended a small hotel just a short distance along the street; his own coaching inn being of an unsavoury reputation. Xavier walked down the darkened, cobbled street which was typical of most cities in this region in that there was only a narrow pathway coming out from the continuous walls of two-story buildings. Occasionally, there would be a railed pretence for a front garden, but mostly the fronts of each dwelling consisted of a featureless, plastered wall broken only by a broad, iron-clad double door and two barred windows on either side. Above on the upper floor, there may be shuttered casement windows or even a small balcony. It seemed a well-established barrio[1] which probably dated well back into the last century.

Eventually he came to a neat, white-washed section of wall which had the usual double door and barred and tightly shuttered windows, but these seemed to be painted in another light colour, which the faint light of a small lantern above the door showed to be a light blue. The sign next to the doorway said in bright red on white 'La Posada de los Niños[2]'

---

[1] suburb
[2] The Inn of the Children

There was a small bell hanging from an ornate curved holder next to the door and despite the late hour, Xavier rang it. Eventually a small 'Judas Hole' viewing hatch slide open and a rough voice asked him his business.

"I am sorry for the lateness of my visit." Xavier apologised "but do you have a room for the night?"

The hatch slide shut and there were the sounds of bolts being slid open. A small wicket gate opened and he was motioned inside. He found that he was in the usual eighteenth-century house with a high archway as the entrance way which led into a spacious open courtyard. There were two doors on either side of the arch; one which was small and had a waist-high counter at its entrance and the other which was open and led into a large room which also had been white washed and was decorated with wall-hangings of brightly-coloured wool and some paintings. There was a long counter on the far side and a small fire was burning in a fireplace in the opposite corner.

The old man who had opened the gate was above the average height for an Andean and his face had obviously seen many a tough day. Never-the-less, there was a welcoming smile on his face as he asked Xavier if he would like something to eat. Xavier had had very little to eat along the last leg of his journey and so he was very glad for the hot plate of beans and corn which the old man had served from a large pot hanging in the fireplace. A small carafe of red wine and some small bread rolls were brought and placed on the table.

The old man returned to the table with a large key and said in his gruff voice:

"This is for room number eight. It is across the courtyard and up the stair, señor. You can fill in all of your particulars in the morning. Good night to you." With that, he left Xavier to finish his meal in the cheerful room and went across the archway to his small bed in the office on the other side.

His meal finished, he left his bowl and glass on the counter before walking outside and across the courtyard. This was of a good size and had a large ornate fountain in its centre and several plants grew in several large brown, decorated pots placed around it. He looked up and saw a multitude of bright stars in the cold sky framed by a colonnade which ran around the courtyard on the upper floor. There was another small lantern below the steps in the corner of the courtyard where he was just able to discern that the first three steps each had a line of writing on them. He bent down and was able to read each line which spelt out a familiar theme which his grandmother had taught him; the code of good behaviour of Tawantinsuyu, the Incan Empire:

Ama sua: Do not steal
Ama llulla: Do not lie
Ama quella: Do not be lazy

This gave him a feeling of comfort and homeliness and he went to his room and had the best sleep for many days.

Xavier awoke with sunlight streaming through the lace curtains of his room. He sat up and looked around at his surroundings which he had so ignobly ignored the night before. It was spacious with a high ceiling typical of buildings of that colonial era. His large bed had been a welcome comfort and there were more woven hangings around the walls; mostly woven tapestries depicting local country life with people, mostly children, llamas and high mountains. He quickly dressed and went down to breakfast and to make the necessary arrangements to stay for several days.

Back in the cheerful dining room of the previous night, he found a rather rotund lady dressed in bright skirts and wearing a traditional q'ipirina[3], that broad, multi-coloured shawl which had a variety of uses from carrying children to covering the head in adverse weather. She had an even broader smile and introduced herself as Señora Rosario, the proprietoress of the inn and wife of Antonio who was presently tending to the garden in the courtyard. Her aged father, Diego, had been the man who had welcomed Xavier the previous night and she commented that he had once been a famous prize-fighter.

There were several young girls helping Señora Rosario in the kitchen from where

---

[3] Pronounced [cor-Rip-pina]

Xavier was served a very hot aromatic cup of coffee, some freshly baked rolls and even English marmalade; a rare treat in these mountains. Whilst eating, he noticed that out in the courtyard, the many large pots were filled with bright flowers in a variety of colours and several fruit trees also grew along one of its sides. Diego was now being helped by several young boys who obviously also worked at the posada. Señora Rosario noticed his attention and came up to his table and said with some pride:

"Diego and I take some of the homeless children off the streets and give them a home and some honest work for later in their life. This is why our little inn is named after the children."

"A most gratifying charity." Xavier said with some admiration and Señora Rosario smiled her broad smile as she took his empty plates from the table.

There was a large map of the city and its surroundings on a far wall. Xavier got up and walked over to it to get an idea about this city which he had not visited before. Quito is at an elevation of 2,850 metres above sea level, it stated boldly at the bottom of the map and is the second highest capital city in the world, as well as being the closest to the equator from whence the name of the country had been derived. It is located in the basin of the Río Guayllabamba on the eastern slopes of Pichincha, an active volcano. He saw from the map that the city stretched out roughly northeast-southwest within the confines of the narrow river valley between the mountains. The ubiquitous red dot was hand-painted on the map which showed him that the inn was situated near the centre of the city on Calle Venezuela[4] not far from the main square; the Plaza Grande.

---

[4] Venezuela Street

The day being a Monday, and a bright sunny day as well, Xavier decided that he would play the tourist by walking down to the main square to take in some of the sights of the city. Outside, he found the street consisted of colonial-era buildings of two or three stories; some with the usual entrance ways like the inn and others with wide shutters at street level. Whilst most were shut, there were some which were now open to reveal a variety of small shops. In the distance, down the slight slope of the street, stood the twin towers of what appeared to be a cathedral.

There were a good number of people now out in the street; some just walking, others browsing at the offerings of the shops and others carrying large bundles or pushing small hand carts. A few carriages also clattered along the centre of the street. His general impression was that of a vibrant city with prosperous people. Several passers-by wished him a 'good day' and he felt some happiness which until then had been lacking in his life.

Xavier walked across the street and into the open gardens of the Plaza Grande. This was an imposing square, well paved with several grassy gardens and many trees around its exterior. In the centre was a small, stone fountain, its bubbling water washing over its upper bowl and cascading down into its deep, hexagonal pond[5].

As was usual in many cities, the square was surrounded by many beautiful colonial buildings. Here in the Plaza Grande, most of the buildings were in a dazzling white. On one side of the square to the southwest stood the cathedral with its imposing stone portico and set well back, its two high bell towers.

---

[5] Today this fountain stands in the southwestern part of the square. The large statue commemorating the heroes of independence was unveiled in 1906, now stands in the centre of the square which was renamed the Plaza de la Independencia in that year.

On the opposite side of the square stood the Archbishop's Palace, a beautiful building consisting of two stories of white-painted stone with a long row of columns supporting Greek-style arches on the upper floor. The walls are whitewashed and a number of wooden balconies further added to the appeal of the palace. Xavier had enquired later about this building when back at his inn and had found that it had been rebuilt 1775 by the Spanish architect Antonio García, who introduced this characteristic European style.

On the adjacent and western side of the plaza stood the imposing Presidential Palace with its government offices. This building was more austere than the Bishop's Palace, with a ground floor of dark stone penetrated by a number of small archways. On the floor above was a row of Greek columns and a balconied story above that with classical arches and tall windows. Opposite this on the far side of the plaza were the Municipal Offices built in colonial-era stone and rather plain in structure, probably to reflect the practical nature of local government. The overall effect of the Plaza Grande and its surrounding buildings was very pleasing to Xavier and so he stopped for a while and sat down on one of the many wooden benches near the central fountain to admire the view.

It was a lovely day and Xavier was enjoying the fresh air coming down from the snow-capped mountains beyond the city and watching the activities of the people passing by. Suddenly there was a single fanfare of a trumpet drawing Xavier's attention to some of the crowd congregating over near the Presidential Palace. Curious, he got up and walked over to the line of people who had now assembled on the edge of the pavement of the plaza facing the Palace. He asked a young man what was happening:

"Why señor, it is the Changing of the Guard. This happens every Monday at eleven. You wait and see! It is a grand event," came the reply.

Xavier moved through the crowd until he found a good vantage point in the front row. He noticed that there were now soldiers holding long lances topped with small pennants of the Ecuadorian flag standing between the columns on the upper floor. They stood at attention, their uniforms of long sky-blue coats, white breeches and knee-high shiny black boots made a striking impression and appealed strongly to Xavier's military training. The cuffs of their coats were bright red as were their collars and there were rows of bright golden clasps across their chests. Their tall blue shakos bore a large golden crest bearing the country's coat of arms.

Below, on the street which he was somewhat amused to note was called Calle Chile, stood a double row of Infantrymen clad in the same uniform. They had marched in from one side behind a small military band. A small group of officers had ridden their horses along the ranks of soldiers and now formed up as a line at one side not far from where Xavier was standing. They looked splendid in their blue dress uniforms with their gold braided epaulettes. Xavier had a deep pang of both pride and sadness when he recalled the many times when he had paraded in Lima with his own cavalry regiment.

Suddenly there was a commotion close at hand. A small barking dog had run across the line of waiting officers and one of the horses had reared up and was now out of control. A new and untrained mount was Xavier's instant thought. The young officer mounted on this horse vainly attempted to reign it in but to no avail. With a sudden jump and kicking of both its hind legs, the horse arched its back and the officer, a young Subteniente[6], fell to the ground. With the horse still kicking its legs and stamping its hooves around the young officer, it would be only a matter of time before he was trampled underfoot. Xavier quickly ran to the horse and grasped its reins; his former military training as a cavalry officer meant that this reaction was sudden and effective. With a few soothing words close to the scared horse's face, he was able to quickly calm her down. Several of the soldiers had broken ranks and were now dragging the young officer away from where he had fallen under the horse's hooves. He appeared to be unhurt but very humiliated by his fall. He looked up at Xavier and gave him a weak smile and a nod of thanks, still too shocked to speak. Xavier handed the reins back to the young man but was suddenly aware of

------

[6] Sub-Lieutenant – the lowest Army officer rank.

another presence nearby. He turned and saw that another horseman had ridden up and was now at his side. Xavier looked up at the tall officer sitting above him on a fine chestnut stallion. This officer wore the epaulettes of a Teniente Coronel who was obviously the Commanding Officer of the regiment. He smiled and extended his hand to Xavier:

"I must thank you most sincerely señor for your quick action in saving my young officer from a trampling. My regiment owes you a debt of thanks."

"I was glad to be of service, Colonel. The poor animal was frightened and acted in the way that it did. I hope that the young man is uninjured," Xavier replied. Taking the colonel's proffered hand.

To answer that question, the young officer walked up to them and, looking somewhat embarrassed, apologised to his commanding officer and also extended his hand to Xavier, saying:

"Yes, thank very much señor for your assistance just then. I am Subteniente José Ayora y Quevedo and I am in your debt."

Xavier smiled at the young man as he took his hand and said softly:

"It happens to many a young officer on such a spirited mount. I was just fortunate enough to be here when it was frightened by that dog."

The young officer thanked Xavier a second time and with two of his men holding the now quietened animal, he mounted with some apprehension and slowly re-joined the group of other officers who would no doubt expect a round of drinks that night in their Mess.

The colonel looked down and asked: "Thank you again, señor for your gentleness with my young José. He is a new officer but comes from a well-connected family of noble background. For all of that he is still an earnest young man and will do well in time."

He took off his shako and wiped his brow. "May I enquire your name, señor? I would like to offer you some reward for your prompt and very brave service this morning.

"Why thank you, Colonel. I am called Xavier Aguirre del Río and I have recently arrived in your lovely country…but no, a reward is not needed for I only did what a man would do in such a circumstance." Xavier replied.

"A man well-trained in the way of horses, I am thinking." The colonel said with a wry look on his face. "If you would like a change in your life, my regiment is looking for a Master-of-Horse, for we have recently lost ours to another regiment. I am Colonel Robles and I would be most gratified to receive you .... say at noon, tomorrow? "The colonel reached down and handed Xavier a card.

"Our barracks are at the Army's Headquarters which is not far from here – we are the Second Regiment of Footguards and I am certain that you would be most welcome, "the colonel said with some enthusiasm. "If you are interested, come to my office at the Headquarters tomorrow, I would like to see if I could reward you in a more practical way."

With that, the colonel turned his horse away and joined the other officers. Xavier pushed back through a welcoming crowd; some patted him on the shoulders and others quietly thanked him for his deed. The military ceremony went on and the band struck up the national anthem which all joined in singing as the huge Ecuadorian flag was hoisted up the flagpole atop the Presidential Palace. Xavier had indeed arrived in the promised land.

Capítulo Cinco:
Nuevos Amigos y Enemigos
(Chapter Five: New Friends and Enemies)

Xavier sat down on one of the stone benches opposite the Presidential Palace and thought of the offer which the colonel had made. The guards had all left the plaza save the two who now stood on either side of the entrance archway. A soft breeze blew gently through the palms and the local people continued to go about their usual business.

He thought for a long time; about the offer and his flight from his father's home in Lima. He had made no plans except to go north into territory which was new to him and he had not thought about what he would do when he found a place to rest. They say that God looks after fools and the saintly, but Xavier felt that he was neither; well, perhaps a fool, but now he was here and an opportunity had presented himself.

He had no doubts that he could easily perform the duties of a 'Master-of-Horse for he was an experienced horseman and his former cavalry unit was very particular in its treatment of its horses. He also would be at home in regimental life, something which he had been trained for at the Academy and experienced over those many years in his rise to Troop Captain. It would, at least give him a time to think in some familiar surroundings and his savings would soon need some replenishment. Yes! He would accept the colonel's generous offer.

Xavier was now in a happy mode and it was if the entire world had been lifted off his shoulders. He walked back down Calle Venezuela to his posada and was greeted by Señora Rosario who was now cooking up an aromatic seco de carne con tamarindo[1], in her kitchen.

---

[1] A beef stew in tamarind sauce, well-known in Ecuador.

"I have been offered a job, Señora!" he said with some pride. "At the Army Headquarters with the Second Guard Regiment."

Señora Rosario turned around from the stove with a huge smile and clasped her hands together:

"Oh, so you have met Colonel Ernesto, then! He is a good man Señor Aguirre, my Antonio was once in the army and served under him at the Battle of Guayaquil. The good Colonel was only a Capitán then, but he looked after his soldiers.... when was that? Ah, now I remember, it was a long time ago, in 1860, I think. How the time passes."

Xavier sat down at the table near the fireplace for the weather had turned cold as it sometimes does in Quito when the wind blows down the valley from the snow-capped mountains. He remembered that year well. As he had just been promoted to Teniente and his father had been very proud of him. Señora Rosario set a bowl of her delicious stew on the table in front of him along with a freshly baked bread roll and, with her usual big smile, returned to her stove.

The next day, Xavier put on his best clothes, polished his boots and with a cheery farewell to Señora Rosario, walked back down the street to the Plaza Grande. He had asked Antonio the previous evening over a bottle good wine where the Military Headquarters was located and found that it was in an imposing white building just west of the Plaza Grande.

Xavier did not have to walk very far until he came to the Military Headquarters. The complex of old colonial buildings, all in white, took up the entire block. There was a high stone and grated wall surrounding the buildings and at each corner there were small guard towers commanding good views down each street. He walked along the street which seemed to be the major thoroughfare until he came to an impressive archway at which a lone sentry stood, rather casually he thought, by a double metal gate. The sentry stood more erect as Xavier approached and attempted to look straight ahead whilst keeping an eye on this approaching stranger.

Xavier came up to the guard and handed him the colonel's card with a brief explanation of the reason for his visit. The sentry looked at the card, returned it and then opened one of the gates, pointing down the wide road which led into the interior of the complex and gave a few words of direction. The headquarters building was apparently not far from the entrance and in one of the buildings on the right which Xavier found formed one side of an impressive quadrangle.

There was a broad stairway leading up to a set of heavy wooden and studded doors above; one of which was open. He entered and an orderly who was sitting at a small desk stood up, came over to him and asked his business with the regiment. Again, Xavier presented the colonel's card and explained the reason for his visit, giving his name as well. He was told to wait whilst the orderly walked over to another door; one which obviously led into another office. He knocked and a voice from inside bade him enter. He returned almost immediately and held the door open for Xavier to enter:

"The Colonel will see you now, Señor Aguirre." He said, and stood at attention when Xavier entered.

Teniente Coronel Ernesto Robles stood up from behind his large and beautifully carved desk. He was an imposing man; tall and well-built with a full head of closely cropped hair in the German fashion and thin, black moustaches. He had a broad face, tanned with many years of campaigning in the field. It was a friendly face with wrinkles at the corners of his eyes which suggested that the broad smile which he now gave was not an uncommon feature of his character.

"Ah, Señor Aguirre!" he said in a deep but friendly voice. "I am delighted that you have considered my offer. Please sit down." He said coming around the desk and bringing a chair from near the wall.

"Thank you, Colonel. Your offer certainly intrigued me and was most welcome considering that I am new to your lovely country and without any immediate prospects."

The colonel returned to his chair behind the desk and looked up and smiled again.

"From your accent, I perceive that you are Peruvian...no matter. Our counties have often bickered about the border which the Spaniards arbitrarily drew across the Indians' land. But that is a matter of politics and I still need a Master-of-Horse if you would work for Ecuador." He said with a slight twinkle in his eye and shrugging his shoulders.

"Benito!" he called out. The orderly opened the door and came in, coming to attention in front of the desk. "Let us have some coffee, please and tell the Adjutant that I would like to see him," he continued and as the orderly turned to carry out the order, he added: "and ask Subteniente Ayora if he wouldn't mind saddling his horse and bringing it around to the parade ground."

The orderly quietly left, closing the door behind him. The colonel put his hands on the desk and looked at Xavier, again with the friendly smile:

"It was obvious from your actions yesterday, Señor Aguirre, that you have had some considerable experience with horses. No one could have quietened such a spirited and frightened animal as fast as you did. Again, I give you my thanks. But tell me, where did you acquire such skills?"

Xavier looked up and for a moment had to think very quickly about what he was about to say. Colonel Ernesto seemed to be a man who was used to dealing with men and liars.

"My father taught me from a very early age, Colonel. On our small estate outside of Lima," he replied. This was the truth as the young Xavier had indeed been with horses since he was a small boy on his parent's estate just outside of the city. He had very fond memories of that time and regretted the time when his father had become the colonel of his own cavalry regiment and had thought it appropriate to move into the city with his family. Of course, his expertise in horsemanship and his deep affection for his horses owed more to his life as a cavalry officer than his early childhood. He had a momentary pang of guilt and loss when he remembered leaving his own cavalry mount Kiyari, back in Peru.

Colonel Ernesto stood up and walked around the side of his desk and placed his broad hand on Xavier's shoulder.

"Well, my good Aguirre! Let us see if you are truly good for my regiment. Come! I have one last test for you."

Xavier stood up and followed the colonel out of his office and through the main door of the headquarters. At the bottom of the stairs, he saw the young Subteniente and his horse from yesterday's parade. The young man recognised Xavier and smiled, lifting his hand up in a smart salute:

"Good morning, señor. It is a pleasant surprise to see you again," he said earnestly.

The colonel walked over to his young officer and said: "Thank you José, I would like to borrow your horse for brief moment to see a little more of Señor Aguirre's horsemanship, if you permit it?"

The young officer quickly handed the reins of his horse to the colonel who then led the horse over to where Xavier was standing.

"Well now, Señor Aguirre! If I may be so bold as to ask you to mount this fine horse – Manuella is her name – and show us a little of your riding style, it would conclude my opinions as to your joining our regiment.

"It would be an honour, colonel." Xavier said with a small nod of thanks to the young officer whose horse he had now been given. He took the reins from the colonel and went up close to the horse's head. He stroked the front of its nose gently and spoke its name several times. With one last caress of his hands, he moved down and grasped the pommel of the saddle, put his foot into the stirrup and deftly mounted the horse.

There was a small riding track which ran down the longer side of the rectangular parade ground. Xavier turned the horse around and gently dug in his heels and put the horse into a gallop down the track, holding his body low along the horses' neck in the style that he was trained to do at 'The Charge'.

At the end of the track, he brought Manuella to a sudden halt. He quickly whirled her around and galloped back towards the two officers. Perhaps it was pride, or the thrill of being in the saddle again, but he then performed one of his most dangerous tricks of horsemanship. This was the famed jigitovka, an act which he had heard that the Russian Cossacks had learned from the Turks. This required the riders to go at full gallop swing one leg over the saddle, jump to the ground with both legs together and then jump back into the saddle. At its most dangerous level, the rider would then also pick-up objects from the ground such as a hat and then ride on. Today, Xavier was content with only mounting and dismounting at the gallop. He reined in Manuella in a cloud of dust just short of the two officers.

The young Subteniente just stood transfixed at the horsemanship which Xavier had just demonstrated and the colonel smiled his enigmatic smile and gave a small round of applause.

"Very impressive, señor, but I doubt that there were any Cossacks on your father's small estate. Still, you are an excellent horseman and I will ask no more questions about your past. I am sure that you will be a very useful Master-of-Horse in my regiment. You will have several grooms and ostlers at your command and I might hope that you can show some of my younger officers some finer arts of caring for their horses." The latter comment he made whilst turning to his young subordinate and giving him a frown then a friendly wink of an eye.

Xavier laughed at that and gave the reins of Manuella back to her owner with a word of thanks. He turned and followed the colonel back into his office.

Standing at the door was an older man with the insignia of a Capitán. He was a tall man of about late middle age – old for his rank – and he had the empty sleeve of his left arm pinned across the front of his service uniform.

"Allow me to name my very able Adjutant, Capitán Antonio Castillo Andrés," the colonel said introducing the officer. "He will tell you that it is really he himself who runs this regiment, but don't listen to him!"

The Adjutant laughed at this comment and said with some laughter still in his eyes: "Why, that is not true, my colonel. I am but your humble servant."

"Bah Antonio! You know that I could not run this group of banditos without your experience and skills." The colonel said laughing as he went into his office.

Inside, he sat down and introduced Xavier to the Adjutant: "Antonio, this is Señor Xavier Aguirre del Río, our new Master-of-Horse. Would you please show him his quarters and explain a little about his duties and about our regiment? Be kind, now! I do not want our new man to feel unwanted. He is also to be afforded the courtesy of membership of the Officers' Mess so introduce him to some of the other officers tonight, will you?"

With that, Xavier knew with some joy that he was now a civilian member of the Second Regiment of Footguards. The Master-of-Horse no less, charged with the duty of the overall charge of the officers' mounts and the few other horses and mules which belonged to the regiment. As he walked through the buildings with the friendly Adjutant, he also found that his duties would include overseeing the men who worked in the small stables and also to assist some of the younger officers with their horsemanship. These would be very light duties compared to those in which he had been trained in the cavalry.

Xavier was shown a room which was at the end of the Officers' Quarters of the barracks. The Adjutant apologised for the austerity of the accommodation which consisted of the small room, about four metres square and having a single bed, wardrobe and a small chair and table which also had a porcelain basin and water jug sitting on top. There was also a row of coat hangers and a small cross on one wall, and a mirror above the table.

The Adjutant shrugged his shoulders and gave Xavier another apologetic look and waved down the hallway with his one arm: "There is the bathroom down the end of the hall and if you put your boots out at night, our batman will clean them for you. The Officers' Mess is upstairs in this building and we dine at eight. I will see you there, yes?"

"Thank you, Capitán Castillo. I will look forward to meeting the other officers tonight."

"Please call me 'Antonio' when we are in informal circumstance and may I call you Xavier?" the Adjutant said, extending his hand. "We are an informal group when it comes to the activities in the mess and Colonel Ernesto is a good commander who is well-loved by his men, as you will find. We are all friends in the mess – well almost!"

Shaking his hand, the Adjutant turned but as the he was about to leave, he turned and slapped the side of his face:

"I am forgetting my duty! I will instruct the Quartermaster to issue you with the usual items – no side arms nor parade uniforms of course, but there will be a set of work clothing, toiletries and the like. Sargento

Primero[2] Narvia is another good man, and he will not skimp when it comes to essential supplies. But be warned, he hates waste and has no problems when addressing criticisms to our younger officers. There will also be a Regimental Identification Card for you at the Orderly Room. Have a good day, my friend."

With a casual salute, the Adjutant left the room leaving Xavier to sit on his new bed and wonder at the speed of his acceptance in this new country. After a while, he stood up and explored his new barracks. The Officers' Quarters consisted of a row of small rooms opening out onto a wide corridor which ran down to a large staircase at its end and another door which opened into a large and well-lit toilet block which contained change rooms, baths and toilets. It was not unlike his own barracks back at his former regiment. It would appear that armies in different countries seem to evolve into the same sort

---

[2] First Sergeant,

of social structure with the same sort of customs and accommodation.

He walked out and around the edge of the Parade Ground – it would not be good to darken his reputation by walking across what was considered to be hallowed ground. He found the stables behind one of the buildings at a short distance from the Parade Ground along one of the many cobble roads which ran this way and that in the complex. They were housed in a modest building consisting of several opened archways which led into the interior which contained separate stalls for the horses and mules with a small courtyard beyond, which was used for exercising the animals. Another building nearby held the carriages and supply carts of the regiment as well as stores of hay and grain. It was an impressive and well-organised system although much smaller than that in his former cavalry regiment. He laughed quietly to himself when he remembered his old prejudiced views that the infantry only thought of horses as a handicap at the best of times and a potential food source at the worse.

He walked slowly back to the Headquarters building and found that the Orderly had already prepared a smart new and impressive identification card which showed him as 'Señor Xavier Aguirre del Río, civilian Master-of-Horse of the Second Regiment of Footguards'. There was the regimental crest with a gold border around the edge of the card. There were also a few lines of fine print below his name requesting all and sundry to afford him the courtesy of an Officer in the Ejército Ecuatoriano – the Army of Ecuador.

Xavier walked back to La Posada de los Niños' feeling very happy with himself. He collected his things from his room and went down and told Señora Rosario about his good fortune and expressed his sadness that he would now have to leave the posada. The fine lady that she was, Señora Rosario thanked him for his short stay and expressed the hope that she would see him out and about in the city and reminded him that there was always a fine guatita[3] at the La Posada de los Niños' whenever he would care to visit. Xavier kissed her pudgy hand and settled his account, giving her a few more of his precious coins than was needed.

Later that day he drew his new set of work clothes and other items from the gregarious Quartermaster, who was a particular friend of the one-armed Adjutant, and had been asked to look favourably on the new man. He brushed down his best items of clothing and gave his boots an additional shine and although it would still be an hour before dinner, he went down the corridor and up the wide staircase to the Officers Mess.

---

[3] Guatita (meaning 'little guts') is Ecuador's national dish, a hearty, thick stew consisting of tripe simmered in a sauce of peanuts and potatoes.

This too seemed to have the universal military style which he had been used to back in his old regiment. There was a set of double glass doors etched with the regimental badge and beyond these a small anteroom with a table and small silver dish for the receiving of visiting officer's personal cards. There was also an ornate, leather-bound guest book, glass ink holder and pen ready for these new guests. On one wall there was a rack of several rows of wooden knobs upon which now several kepis were hanging showing him that he would not be alone in the mess at this early hour. He hung his modest cap on one of the lower knobs; it looked very out of place with the navy blue and gold kepis which also hung there. Xavier was yet unsure of his current status so ignored the guestbook and opened the inner glass doors as he walked into the Officers' Mess.

Inside he found a large and elegant room with tall windows on one side which he found later overlooked the Parade Ground. At the far end was a large and elaborate fireplace at which an orderly was now arranging some pieces of timber so that it would be alight for the cool night and the evening meal. Above the fireplace hung a portrait of the current President of Ecuador, Juan Espinosa, between the flags of Ecuador and the Regimental Colours. In front of this was a long table which stretched to almost the entire width of the room. Two other long tables flanked this head table at right-angles forming a large U-shaped configuration taking up the lower third of the room. The rest of the room had arrangements of comfortable lounge chairs, small tables and the ubiquitous potted palms. There was a large wooden bar set around the corner of the room closest to the entrance and above it were many crests and pennants which belonged to visiting military units.

Xavier stood at the inner doors and looked around the room. There were several officers singly, or in small groups, sitting in the chairs talking quietly in the centre of the room. All were dressed in their formal evening uniforms of dark blue coats with high collars, matching blue trousers, and red sashes to match the single red strip down the sides of their trousers. Their knee-high black boots were highly polished and their gold braid sparkled in the light of the many candles set in ornate silver candelabras around the room. Xavier felt somewhat shabby in his best civilian clothes and he thought back to the days of his old mess where his elegant cavalry uniform would easily be more than a match for such sartorial splendour.

To his right he saw a small group of officers standing at the bar. They had all turned and now looked at him with some curiosity and a little distain at this civilian interloper in

their midst. Suddenly one of the officers
pushed his way through the group and
strode over to where Xavier was standing; it
was the young Subteniente, José Ayora.

"Welcome to our humble mess, Señor
Aguirre! "he said with a broad smile and
extended his hand. "Come! Let me introduce
you to some of my brother officers; all good
fellows each and every one. I have been
telling them of your prowess with my horse
this morning"

The young officer had taken Xavier by the
arm and now escorted him over to the group
standing at the bar. They made way for him
to come up to the high wooden structure and
whilst the looks of distain had vanished,
those of curiosity had remained.

Ayora slapped Xavier on the back and said
to his friends with some good-natured pride:

"Allow me to name Señor Xavier Aguirre del Río, our new Master-of-Horse; the man who saved my skin and pride at the last Changing-of-the-Guard."

This introduction suddenly changed the mood of the group who now slapped Xavier on the back or shook his hand. A tall man with blonde hair and pale skin stepped forward and shook Xavier by the hand. He was obviously of European extraction and had a small scar running down the side of his cheek. His epaulettes showed that he held the rank of Mayor[4]. He smiled at Xavier and said in heavily accented Spanish:

"Indeed, Señor Aguirre! Let me welcome you to our mess. Do not listen to the young Ayora. We are not as 'humble' as he would have you to believe, but we are all brother officers and friends here. Allow me to introduce myself as the Ritter von

---

[4] Major

Königsbau, for my sins, President of the Mess and very late of the army of the King of Bavaria" he said with some gentle, self-depreciating laughter. "Welcome to our happy company".

Another major stepped forward and put his hand on the big German's arm: "Mayor Karl here is indeed our well-loved President and a good friend of Colonel Ernesto, but be warned! He will tell you many a story about his blood-thirsty days fighting in Europe. Don't believe them! That evil-looking scar on his face came from a student duel which was almost mandatory at their crazy university."

There was a lot of good-natured laughing at this comment and Mayor Karl smiled and bowed to his fellow officers. Another officer, a Capitán reached through the crowd and gave Xavier a large and ornate crystal glass of red wine. More glasses were handed around from the grinning steward behind the bar.

"Gentlemen! Here's to the new member of this august Regimental Mess and Master-of-Horse, Señor Xavier Aguirre del Río!" the captain announced loudly. The glasses were all raised and drunk in one motion. Xavier felt that he had indeed found a new home.

Mayor Karl lent over and gave Xavier a wink and said in a conspiratorial tone: "Back home in Bavaria, we would have now thrown all of the glasses into the fireplace, but here in Ecuador they cannot afford the expense!" More laughter.

Subteniente Ayora elbowed his way through the senior officers and again took Xavier by the arm: "The Colonel will be here soon, so let me show you some of our mess," he said, steering Xavier across the mess and between several clusters of chairs and potted palms.

"Here is our Billiard Room," he said, sweeping his free arm across the entrance to a small archway which led into another room on the wall opposite to the windows. It was larger than Xavier had first imagined and contained two billiard tables and their fittings. The walls were huge with paintings of several battle scenes from South America's wars of independence.

Next door to this was another archway which led into a room of the same size as the first but was completely free of furniture. There were several mats on the floor and racks of exercising equipment and swords arranged around the room. They had interrupted a bout of fencing which had been going on in one corner of the room. Two men now stood with their white padded jackets, metal-gridded face masks and foils by their sides looking at the intruders. One quickly removed his mask and came over to where Xavier and Ayora were standing. He was a thin man and also of equal rank to Ayora but a little older. His jet-black hair was neatly cut and oiled as was his thin moustache. There was a slight sneer to his lips as he said:

"Ah, so this must be our new Master-of-Horse!" there was no friendliness in his tone and no hand extended in friendship. Instead, he quickly threw the handle of his foil across to Xavier and added:

"If you are a gentleman, let us see how you handle the sword." He handed Xavier his mask and went over to the other man and quickly pulled off his mask and snatched away his foil.

Xavier looked at Ayora blankly who lent close to his face and whispered: "This is Subteniente Carrasco Flores, our 'rotten apple' as the English would say."

Flores returned with his fencing mask on and his foil in his arms. Xavier, who had been his regimental fencing champion decided that now was not the time to demonstrate any skill in this sport so he held his foil out by the handle and said:

"My apologies señor, I really am not much of a swordsman and so I must ask to be excused from your generous offer of competition."

Flores did not remove his mask but took up the 'en garde' position and said aggressively: "Nonsense! A gentleman should always know how to defend himself with a sword. Let us see if you are a gentleman or not!"

Xavier could no longer avoid this confrontation, so he put the mask over his head and took up what he hoped would be a very clumsy 'en garde' stance. Flores made a quick feint to draw Xavier in but he stood his ground without moving from his awkward-looking position. Flores then made a quick lunge and although the blades were capped, Xavier could not let it strike his chest so he moved his foil awkwardly across his body and deflected Flores' blade. A return lunge or riposte was normally expected but Xavier again stood his ground. Another lunge and yet another awkward parry. It was now obvious that Flores' patience had gone and he took a quick step backward and then rapidly advanced for another, more powerful lunge.

Xavier had noted that Flores was not the skilled swordsman that he pretended to be as his grip on his foil was too casual. Usually, the foil's pistol grip is held further forward in the hand, being held lightly by the fingers alone but Xavier noticed that Flores held the grip butted against his hand and so was held loosely between the fingers and the top of the palm.

When the angry lunge came, it came at a high angle and Xavier expertly took it on his blade and quickly twisted his wrist so that his blade twisted around that of his opponent and flicked it out of his grasp in a parry known as 'Contre Quarte'. The foil fell silently onto the mat.

Flores, now unarmed, quickly ripped off his masked and glared malevolently at Xavier who assumed a dumb visage and reached down to pick up the fallen sword.

"Oh dear! I am sorry señor. Please forgive my awkwardness but I am not used to such exercise." He said, handing the foil, handle first, to his opponent. "Thank you for your attempt to teach me some of your gentlemanly skills."

With that, he turned to Ayora who had an uncertain smile on his face and they both left

the room. He had made some good friends
that evening but also an enemy.

Capítulo Seis:
La Historia del Sacerdote
(Chapter Six: The Priest's Story)

And so, Xavier's life with the regiment began. He found that his work was not taxing compared to his previous regimental duties in the cavalry; now he only had to help a few horsemen with their relatively gentle horses. Training the horses to be insensitive to loud sounds which simulated battle and then training their riders to remain in the saddle was not difficult for him.

Life in the Officers' Mess was generally enjoyable and he found that he was well accepted, although he stayed away from the gambling tables and moderated his drinking habits. Life for some of the younger officers could be hazardous and expensive. He made several good friends amongst the officers, especially the young Subteniente José Ayora and the one-armed Adjutant; the aggressive

Subteniente Flores he managed to avoid. That was not hard to do as Flores seemed to be unpopular with most of the other officers except one or two sycophantic Subtenientes who seem to be attracted to his family connections and the generosity of his purse. Colonel Ernesto proved to be a popular commanding officer and was usually a guest of the mess on most nights; commanding officers not being part of the mess itself and usually were required by etiquette to ask permission of the Mess President to enter.

It was now Xavier's first Sunday with the regiment and, as was the custom, it was a 'make-and-mend' day in which the soldiers could get on with their own private tasks, play a little sport and relax in their own messes. The only requirement that day was the usual Church Parade which occurred as a private Mass at ten in the morning. This meant that the men were to be in their best uniforms – not the highly decorative Guard uniform worn for the Changing of the Guard – but their best parade uniform of dark blue jacket with red facings and matching kepi, white riding breeches and highly polished black boots.

The barracks did have its own small chapel set in one corner of the Parade Ground opposite the Headquarters Building, but it could not contain the full regiment of over six hundred men and was only for private use such as Confession. It also held the Regimental flags and was the resting place of former commanding officers.

Church Parade was held outside of the barracks and so at about nine-thirty, the men would leave the barracks in small groups to go to church. Xavier noted that Colonel Ernesto had instituted this behaviour as a break from their usual formal regimental parade manoeuvres. This added to the social relaxation of the holiday. It also gave the men a chance to interact with the local community; to buy a few empanadas from the old lady who had the small street stand near the Plaza Grande, or simply to sit in the plaza with the old men and talk of older times.

Xavier walked out of the barracks gate with his young friend José and was surprised when they walked past the Plaza Grande and not across to the cathedral on its far side. Instead, they continued to follow the other small groups of soldiers along Calle Garcia Moreno past several beautiful colonial stone buildings until they came to a small brown church façade. As he looked up, he saw that this façade was only a small part of a much larger building which was painted in dazzling white which extended along most of the street to the far corner. Here, the building rose in an elegant bell tower topped with a crucifix.

"This is La Iglesia de la Compañía de Jesús[1]" José said with some pride, waving his arm across the expanse of the building. Our regiment has had a long connection with the Jesuits, even after they were expelled in 1767. Now that they have returned, we attend their Mass."

Xavier was well aware that the Jesuits had been expelled from South America because in Europe and here in South America, they were considered to have too much influence, especially in political matters. The Jesuits also wanted to raise the moral level of the ordinary people which meant that some members of the ruling classes would have to reform their lives and stop exploiting the common people, especially those of the indigenous tribes. Moreover, the Jesuits owed their allegiance directly to the Pope and not to the hierarchy of the local church authorities who often had connections with

---

[1] The Church of the Company of Jesus – the Jesuit church.

the some of the ruling families. It was not until the new political changes had swept through Europe after the Napoleonic wars and the surge of nationalism and independence in South America that the Society of Jesus was reinstated. José had explained that things had moved slowly due to the political turmoil which was in Ecuador at the time, so the Jesuits did not return there until 1862.

They went inside and Xavier was immediately struck by the ornate beauty of the interior. Everywhere the walls and the interior arches along their sides were covered with a spectacular pattern or ornamentation of brown etched in gold. There were small paintings of the saints on each arch column. Beyond the archways, the richly decorated walls also contained niches each with carvings of the saints in dark wood. The ceiling was also decorated in a finer more intricate pattern of gold. The first impression that Xavier had was that the overall Baroque style was also heavily influenced by Moorish design. The overall effect was most stunning. Xavier could only wonder about the lavishness of the interior of the church and the effect that such a rich mixture of design would have on the common man.

José led him down the central aisle of the church which was already crowded with the men of the regiment. It had been a long-standing custom for this Mass to be held at this time, separately from the other times for Mass for the rest of the church's congregation. Xavier felt some pride for this regiment, now all dressed in their blue and red uniforms and sitting in silence waiting for the service to start. Xavier walked down the aisle, gave a short bow to the altar and sat in the fourth row which had been reserved for the most junior officers. Colonel Ernesto, as was appropriate, sat in the first row on the right aisle seat.

Two young acolytes in their white vestments moved quietly around the sanctuary, straightening the altar cloth, lighting the candles and arranging the sacraments in the large tabernacle which sat in the centre of the altar. Their ministrations complete, they quickly left the sanctuary leaving the church and its uniformed congregation in silent prayer.

Colonel Ernesto had been occasionally turning and watching the entrance to the church. He now stood up as a sign that his regiment should also do so. The Processional Hymn came in the form of a Gregorian chant as the small group came down the nave from behind them. It consisted of only the two acolytes who now acted as Thurifer and

Crucifer[2] with the priest who followed them down the central aisle. He was a very old man who walked with a jerky step that communicated great energy. His nose and chin were angular and his eyes twinkled with shrewdness and a love of life.

Xavier had never been to a Mass which was celebrated by a Jesuit priest before and so he was interested to see how it differed from his own concept of the Mass from his childhood days and from his old regiment's Church Services. He did not consider himself a deeply religious man nor one having much knowledge of church affairs, but he had a basic belief in God and accepted what was celebrated in the mass, even if it was mainly as part of church ritual.

The Mass began and Xavier found that it followed the usual format with which he was

---

[2] The altar servers carrying the incense burner and tall cross respectively.

familiar. Colonel Ernesto took the first reading of the New Testament, Mayor Karl took that of the Old Testament and lastly Capitán Antonio, the one-armed Adjutant, took the second New Testament reading. These were from Luke 15: verses 11 to 32; Leviticus 25:25–37; and Acts 9:1-22 respectively. Xavier paid little attention to these readings as he had heard many readings during his church services; sometimes they were well-known stories and were interesting in themselves but their meaning often was not lasting. Instead, he looked around at the beautifully ornate church and admired the work that went into its construction and the thought which must have gone into its conception.

The old priest slowly stepped up into the pulpit and looked down at his assembled congregation and smiled.

"Today's sermon is about redemption – something that all soldiers must at one time seek from our Father."

There were a few low chuckles from some of the uniformed congregation as some of the men remembered times when they had needed help and redemption from a variety of earthly sins. Xavier was suddenly struck by the old man's presence, for his voice was firm and strong; precise in its pronunciation and sincere in its tone. Here was a man who would attract anyone's attention. Xavier's attention too was now focused on the old priest's words as the sermon progressed.

At the start, the old priest reminded the congregation that the parable of the Prodigal Son was the third and final parable of the cycle relating to redemption; following the parable of the Lost Sheep and the parable of the Lost Coin.

The priest paused for a moment and looked over his spectacles at his congregation and smiled: "As I recall, it was the Jewish philosopher Philo who observed that parents often do not lose thought for their wastrel children.... In the same way, God too...takes thought also for those who live a misspent life, thereby giving them time for reformation, and also keeping within the bounds His own merciful nature."

Some of the men chuckled at the priest's suggestion that some of them may also be wastrels. Xavier thought of his own life and his recent breakdown in the relationship with his own father. This became more apparent as the old priest continued, this time not from the Scriptures but from what he called the Mahayana Buddhist Lotus Sutra. This described a similar story to that told in Luke's Gospel, but here the poor son does not recognize the rich man as his father and he panics when the father sends out the attendants to welcome him, fearing some kind of retribution. Now the rich father gradually draws the son back without divulging their relationship and employs him in successively higher positions until it is time to tell him of their kinship in the end. For Xavier, the personal message was one of redemption, but it would take time until he could resolve his differences with his own father. He hung his head and regretted his flight from his home and hoped that one day he would be restored to his family.

Xavier looked up as the old priest continued his sermon with many references to other religious works. He spoke of the meaning of the words *redemption* and *salvation,* referring to the Latin root meaning 'to be whole.' He spoke of the myths from the ancient Mesopotamia cults with death and rebirth with redemption as the enduring promise. He suggested that it was important to observe whether or not it was in such myths or later in the intercessions and lives of Christ, or those even of Islam's prophet Muhammad, that redemption is achieved not by ideas or doctrines but through the lives and the sacrifices of individuals.

Xavier could feel this message of redemption through personal struggle with God's intercession striking home. The sermon was not delivered in a high tone of academic learning, which he had often heard from churchmen who were proud of some little learning which they had, but from a man who knew what he was talking about. He seemed to talk from personal experience enriched with a deep understanding of the wisdom of others from many lands and from many philosophies. This old priest seemed to live the words which he spoke and now, what he spoke was a comfort to Xavier who was entranced by the old priest's knowledge, conviction and strength of his delivery.

Xavier had never been what others would call a 'religious man'. He went to Mass with his parents when he was younger and usually fidgeted whilst hoping that the sermon would finish soon or annoyed his younger sister who was usually the vision of absolute piety. As a young man at the Academy, he went through all of the usual rituals necessary to show that he would become a good officer and on rare occasions took some note of those sermons which had any relevance to his existence. He always felt that most priests were adequate for their work and some could also be considered wise and holy whilst others revelled in their superior intellect and knowledge of the Bible. The latter he believed went on to become 'Princes of the Church' whilst the former often made good village padres.

It was perhaps several days later when he heard a gentle knocking at his door. He had taken dinner in the Officers' Mess as usual but had retired to his small room early, resolved to write a letter to his father to again explain why he had left the Army and his family. It would be a very difficult and emotional task but one which he felt was long overdue. Xavier got up from his narrow cot and opened the door. To his surprise he found the old priest standing alone in the corridor.

"Forgive me, my son if it is an inconvenient time, but I felt that I should pay our new recruit a social call." He said with that same gentle smile which Xavier had remembered from the Mass on the previous Sunday.

"No Father!" he stammered. "You are most welcome. Please come in."

The old priest came into the room and sat down on Xavier's bed and looked up. "You see, I am an old man and need to take advantage of any place of rest" he said with humour in his quiet voice. "Come sit beside me."

Xavier sat down on the end of the bed and looked at the old priest. In the pulpit he had been a powerful figure; full of energy which swept across the entire congregation. Here, he looked like an old country priest, tired from a hard day's work in the field amongst his flock.

"Permit me to name myself as Father Leontxo Domènech i Casals, to use my full title, but everyone simply calls me 'Father Leon'." It was an unfamiliar name that Xavier thought may have come from the Basque region of Spain.

"Thank you, Father." Xavier exclaimed. "I cannot say that I have much to do with your order."

"No, my son. We tend to be in missions, schools and universities, not as padres of Regiments of Foot. But I am an old Jesuit..." He gave a short laugh. ".. and my superiors thought that I would make a good military padre in my old age. And besides, it was a convenient way of getting rid of me." Another short laugh.

"It was to the Regiment's benefit as I could see from your Mass last Sunday," Xavier replied hoping to give a little comfort to the old priest.

"Ah! Never mind the ramblings of an old man.... let alone a discarded Jesuit. But what of you my son? I only know you as Señor Xavier Aguirre del Río, our new Master-of-the-Horse. For you I am the Regimental Chaplain and am at your service if you should have any troubles in your heart."

Xavier thought for a moment, stood up and walked over to the other side of the room, avoiding the old priest's gaze. "No father, I am quite content," he lied. "The Regiment has given me a new home." Which was the truth.

The old priest looked over his spectacles at Xavier and said with a twinkle in his old grey eyes: "You know, most people think that we Jesuits are like grocers and scholars; we weigh everything and know too much for our own good. Perhaps they are right to think that, but I see in front of me a man who is a little out of place." The old priest also stood up slowly for he no longer had the agility of his youth.

"Come, the night is young even if my poor legs are not. Would you do an old man the courtesy of walking him home to his longings? I have a small cell within the buildings of our church near the Plaza

Grande and the streets of Quito can be dangerous at night. I can promise you a good glass of Aguardiente[3] to keep the cold of the night at bay on your return home." He laughed.

Talking his cap and cloak from behind the door, Xavier opened the door and helped the old man out into the corridor.

It was but a short walk along the narrow, darkened streets, but there was a cold wind blowing from the northeast down off the mountains. As they passed the Plaza Grande, its lamps gave little comfort and at this hour no one sat on its benches. They continued their slow walk along Calle Garcia Moreno, past the Presidential Palace and down the

---

[3] Considered the national drink of Ecuador, Aguardiente is made from fermented sugar cane juice, and leaves an unmistakable burning sensation all the way down the throat and chest after a strong shot.

street until they came to the ornate façade of the Iglesia de la Compañía de Jesús.

They walked past the church and entered through a small gate in the side street. A door to the left of the main church entrance was open and the old priest motioned Xavier to enter. Xavier was again struck by the ornate interior of this church as they walked along the highly polished wood inlaid floor past the golden ornate twisted columns, religious painting and the contrasting dark timber of separate Confessionals. There was a small door in the side wall just past the altar which the old priest opened and went in. Xavier followed and found himself in a small corridor, only slightly less ornate than the nave which he had just left. This opened out onto a long, walled veranda which with a small courtyard beyond. Stone steps led down into the court where there were fruit trees and fragrant bushes growing. A brazier burnt brightly in the middle of the stone veranda which was covered with beautiful blue and red tiles. Several small doors opened out onto the veranda and these Xavier assumed were probably the living quarters of any resident priests and brothers. There were several comfortable armchairs positioned along the veranda and one in particular, with large, soft cushions had been placed near the brazier. The old priest pulled up another armchair and motioned for Xavier to be seated.

He went to a large, ornately-carved cupboard which stood against the wall between two of the doors and opened it. Xavier was astounded to see that it contained many neatly racked bottles of wine and a top shelf containing several silver chalices. The old priest took out one of the bottles and two chalices, similar to those used in Holy Communion.

The old priest gestured with his open hand at the brazier and the cupboard: "We Jesuits take a personal vow of poverty, but that does not mean that the Company[4] suffers any discomfort." He laughed. "Our church factotum, Diago looks after me very well and he knows that I like to sit out here of an evening. Come, sit with me and I will tell you of what I think…if you can take an old man's humble observations"

Xavier walked over and sat down in the proffered armchair. He was now curious about this old priest who did seem to have a deep wisdom and insight into his fellow man.

"Forgive me for prying and being too personal, but …" he put his two hands together as though in prayer…." that is my job and I have done it for such a long time

---

[4] Father Leon often used the common alternative name, 'the Company' when referring to his order, the Society of Jesus.

that I am now sensitive to those who seemed troubled. You see I have been a priest for too many years and I have had a long interest in Natural Philosophy - what modern scholars are now calling 'science'. The use of observation, deduction and logic have always been my passion; some would say part of my vanity, but I try to keep such defects in Human frailty at bay."

He opened the bottle carefully as though it was the last bottle left and poured generous amounts of its rich red contents into the two chalices. "I will give you some of our Aguardiente to see you home later, but first we will have a smooth Rioja wine from my homeland near Bilbao in northern Spain." He said with a smile as he sat down in his chair by the brazier. "So, Señor Aguirre, what do I see in you?" the question was a rhetorical one and the old priest again looked over his spectacles at Xavier and continued.

"I see a military man; most certainly an officer of some note. What were you? A Mayor[5]?"

"No Father, just a Capitán." Xavier answered quietly. He felt that this old priest could look into his very soul and so submitted to his scrutiny.

"I thought this was the case because of your personal habits; the neatness of your dress and the shine of your boots. Also, I have observed you in the Officers' Mess and on the Parade Ground and you seem very much at ease…'home' if I should use a more appropriate word. I also think that from your skills with the horses, and their riders, that you probably came from the Cavalry. Am I correct?"

"Yes, Father. That is so, but please continue as I am fascinated by your deductions.

---

[5] Major

"Thank you, my son. It is one of the few skills left to me outside of this church and the seminary where I once taught logic and natural philosophy. You are, of course a Peruvian. I knew that from your accent and the use of some terms such as '¡Qué roche![6]' which I heard you say one night in the Mess. Moreover, whilst you have most of the features of our European ancestors, there is something about your cheekbones and the angle of your nose which I suggest may indicate some, shall we say, more local heritage?"

"Again, you are right, Father. My grandmother was of the Aymara people but my father insisted that we were of pure European stock."

"Well then, so you speak the Aymara aru – the 'ancient language'! And do you speak Quechua also?"

---

[6] Peruvian slang for 'what a shame' – literally 'What a rock!'

"Only a little." Xavier replied. "There are some similarities but only because in many parts of my country, both languages are spoken."

"Well, then. I must expand your knowledge of the Runasimi[7] as I have not had much chance to use it of late. However, I must warn you that you will speak it with a northern accent!" he laughed.

"But tell me, Capitán Aguirre, why are you here? Did you desert the army?" the old priest suddenly asked.

Xavier was momentarily taken aback by this direct question and moved uncomfortably in his chair. "No Father Leon, I resigned my Commission." This was a painful admission but he somehow felt relieved that he could confide in another person about the pain he

---

[7] This is the term used by the Quechua peoples for their own language and comes from the Quechua terms 'runa 'for 'people' and 'simi' for 'speech,'

felt in leaving his past life behind. He put down his wine and told the old priest of the conflict which he had felt in taking his Troop against his grandmother's people and of the subsequent rejection by his father. The old priest listened in silence whilst Xavier made his confession.

"There are times my son, when one has to do what he feels is right rather than to simply obey what is expected of him." The old priest said as he refilled Xavier's chalice.

Xavier sat in silence for a while, watching the flames flicker through the ironwork of the brazier. He felt as though a large burden had been taken from his shoulders. He put down his wine and settled back into the soft embrace of the armchair and smiled.

"But what of you, Father Leon? What brings a Basque to this far land of the Americas?"

"Ha! You want my confession too, do you Señor Aguirre del Río? Well first you must liberate another good bottle from our stock!" he said pouring the last of the bottle into Xavier's chalice.

The old priest settled back into his armchair and held up his wine in mock salute and began his story: "Well! As you can guess from my full name, I am a native of the northern part of Spain near the Pyrenees but what we Basques' call the Euskal Herria. We speak a different language and have different customs. We have wanted our own freedom for many years, but Madrid always says no!"

The old priest sat quietly for a moment then looked up at Xavier. "Forgive me, my son. I am getting too political. Have you been to Bilbao, Xavier?"

"No Father. My parents took me to Europe when I was a teenager and naturally, we visited Spain as well as a number of other countries, but not to the Basque country."

The old priest sighed and rested back into his chair. He spoke of his early life in his native land and how he had been brought up as the second son of a rich merchant of that beautiful city. His father had many interests in Spain, especially in the north and in Catalonia, around the Mediterranean and beyond. Thinking to pass on some of his business acumen and interests, his father had often taken the young Leontxo with him on many of his trading expeditions, leaving his older brother back in Bilbao to run the family business.

Xavier was very interested to hear of the old priest's travels, as he had not travelled very much himself, other than a brief visit to Europe with his father when he was but a teenager. In particular, he was interested in the circumstances that would turn a young man from a wealthy family into a priest.

The old man continued the story of his travels to the Middle East and then into India and Burma where his father had been trading in silks and spices. In Cairo they had stayed for over a year trading in fine Egyptian cotton and the young man had taken an interest in the beliefs of the local people. He had been taken 'under the wing' by their local agent who had shown him many of the ancient monuments and temples of the old Egyptians and had explained many of their religious and cultural beliefs. The young man had also been interested in the modern religious beliefs of the people of Cairo and had been allowed to study Arabic and the Holy Qur'an at the Central Mosque. He had also befriended a local Rabbi from the old Ben Ezra Synagogue with whom he had often discussed the Hebrew Scriptures and their relationships to his own Christian upbringing.

In Asia, on another extended trip with his father, the young scholar had taken an interest in the Hindu scriptures, notably the Bhagavad Gita and for some time also had studied at a Buddhist monastery. The old priest finished his story and put his chalice gently down on the table and leant back into his chair with a sigh:

"So, you see, my son. It was not hard for me to look at my life from a religious point of view when we finally returned to Bilbao. I had never had much enthusiasm for the trading of cloth but I did have a great interest in the relationship between God and Man, so I became a Jesuit."

"You did not have a sudden religious experience, then?" Xavier asked with just a little cynicism.

The old priest looked up and laughed. "No, my son. It was something which I felt was needed in my life although I did feel that God was beside me when I finally made up my mind."

"And your family?" Xavier enquired.

"Well, my father was not happy. He saw everything in terms of profit and loss and percentages rather than the deeper riches of the Human soul. My mother on the other hand, understood why I wanted to become a priest and eventually my father agreed – at least it would add some piety to the family name."

"But tell me, Father Leon, you seem to know much about local languages and customs. When did you come to Ecuador? The Jesuits have only returned in the last few years."

The old priest smiled and lifted his chalice once more, sat back in his chair once more and looked out at the garden beyond the wall of the veranda.

"Ah! Now when was it? Ah! It was early in 1824 and I had been ordained for only two years when I went on my first visit to South America. The Liberator, Bernardo O'Higgins had invited a delegate from the Holy See to come to Chile to help with the development of the Church there. Cardinal Giovanni Mastai, who later became Pope Pius IX, was Auditor or legal representative assisting the Apostolic Nuncio – the diplomat of the current Pope - who was sent on that mission. I accompanied the delegation to assist but in reality, I was sent by my superiors of the Society to see how the political attitude towards us had changed. Unfortunately, when we got to Santiago, the Liberator had been deposed by yet another general who was not well disposed to the Church, so our mission failed and the rest of the delegation returned to Rome."

"Returning to Rome would have been a big disappointment for you and the Church." Xavier said, as the old priest poured the last to refill his chalice.

The old priest emptied the last of the wine and looked up with that now familiar enigmatic smile. "Ah, but I did not leave. In Chile I fell in with a certain senior member of the Franciscan Order who took pity on me and also wanted my learning for one of their missions further north. So, when our ship docked at Guayaquil, I outwardly became a Franciscan brother and travelled into the interior of the country to help on one of their missions in the mountains. It was a great experience and I learned many of the customs and languages of the people there – including the Quechua language."

The old priest produced the promised bottle of the fiery Aguardiente and took two small glasses from the top shelf of the cupboard. "But that is another story, for it is now time for an old man to take his rest and I must send you once more out into the night"

Capítulo Siete:
Para Mayor Gloria de Dios
(Chapter Seven: *Ad Maiorem Dei Gloriam*[1])

As the year passed, Xavier saw a lot of Father Leon. He found the old priest's company a welcome diversion for the regularity of his daily routine as the regiment's Master-of-Horse.

There also had been a few changes in the regiment; his good friend Subteniente José Ayora had been promoted to a full Teniente and the obnoxious Subteniente Carrasco Flores had not. Coronel Ernesto had approved the latter's application to accept a position of Liaison Officer with the Diplomatic Corp, which no doubt was more in line with the young officer's political ambitions. Both the colonel and most of the officers of the regiment were glad of his departure.

---

[1] 'For the Greater Glory of God' – the Motto of the Jesuits

Xavier was now a well-liked member of the regiment, despite his civilian status. He spent much of his free time with the old priest and his two friends José Ayora and the one-armed Adjutant, Capitán Antonio Castillo. The latter was one of the most courteous of men who carried out his duties as Adjutant with care and consideration regardless of having lost his arm during the Battle of Guayaquil during Ecuador's civil war ten years previously.

The young José Ayora had matured somewhat with his new responsibility as a Platoon Commander and now had the confidence to discuss important issues with Xavier, Father Leon and Capitán Antonio.

Xavier had often walked the old priest back to his quarters at the Jesuit church and had often stayed for some time over a good bottle of wine which the Society seemed to have in good supply. There were other priests who lived in the church precinct but they usually kept to themselves. The incumbent priest lived separately, acting as the assistant to the Father Provincial, the head of the Jesuits in Ecuador who had his own Palacio elsewhere in the city.

Father Leon had a reputation as a shrewd observer of Humankind and had spent several years studying the new applications of deductive reasoning whilst a priest in Europe following the restoration of the Jesuits. One night over a good bottle of wine, Father Leon explained the main principles of deductive reasoning which had he had learned from the writings of such men as Aristotle, Ibn al-Haytham, Francis Bacon and Rene Descartes. Their work, he explained, was the basis for the new system of natural enquiry which he called the 'scientific method'.

The padre soon had an opportunity to demonstrate his understanding of this deductive reasoning. On one of his visits to the regiment's Officers' Mess, Xavier, José and Antonio were sitting together prior to dinner discussing this very topic when a civilian was ushered into the room by the President of the Mess, Major von Königsbau.

"Now Padre, here is your chance to show us some of your skills," said the Adjutant, leaning across the table and nodding to the new arrivals.

The others turned and looked towards the entrance to the mess. The man accompanying Major von Königsbau was tall, thin and dressed in an ill-fitting grey coat. His hair, like the major's was fair and his face was deeply tanned and of a rugged appearance. The observers watched as the two men walked over to the small bar nearby and obtained their drinks before finding another table a short distance from where they were sitting. The President of the Mess gave a slight smile and a quick nod of his head in the Germanic style as they passed.

"So! What do you think, Padre?" The Adjutant said with the mischievous twinkle in his eye which he often had when some devilish idea had come into his head. "A relative of the good Ritter, perhaps?"

The old priest looked across at his tempter and smiled. "No indeed I think not, my son. But I shall give you my observations so that you may learn something other than filling in regimental forms. Firstly, I agree with you that he is a European due to his height which is over the usual for our South American people and his fair hair is more typical of northern Europeans. He is also thin and lacks the breadth of chest of any Andino.

You may also have noticed that there were some minor difficulties with language as they entered. Mayor Karl had to move his head several times to hear our visitor repeat what he had said, and that Spanish is obviously not his first language. English, I should think. Some of the lip movements were not Germanic which is Mayor Karl's first language and I also have a good knowledge of that language having spent many years in Berlin where the Society was retained during its general expulsion elsewhere in Europe. His coat also has an English cut about it as I have travelled in that country also and his long face and thin nose also suggests one from that country.

As to his profession, I would say that he is a Naval Officer. You see that his coat is ill-fitting, suggesting that he is unused to wearing civilian dress. Moreover, as he walked into the room, he did so erect but with what is called a 'rolling gait' – a short stride with the feet well apart suggesting long experience on the heaving deck of a ship. This is also suggested by his face which has long been exposed to the elements. The deep tan, very atypical of his race probably came from a career in tropical waters. Did you notice what drink he ordered at the bar?"

"No why Padre, was it a clue also?" said young José who was totally absorbed in the old priest's account.

"It was a gin!" said the Adjutant who also had a quick mind and was also involved in purchasing the supplies for the bar.

"And the small bottle which Enrique our Steward also gave him?" said the old priest, in a rhetorical manner. "It was probably a bottle of tonic water – so a 'gin and tonic' was ordered.

"What would that suggest?" Xavier asked, keen to find every detail of the old priest's reasoning.

"Gin and tonic is a common English drink partaken by the British in India, their Asian domain. The gin for obvious reasons of sociability and the tonic to ward off malaria which is common in that part of the world also." He continued with his observations and their deductions.

"His age, which is neither young nor old suggests a man of senior rank. As he is alone, I might suggest that of Naval Captain. So! I have to ask myself why would an Englishman of the Royal Navy come to Ecuador and be a guest in a mess of an infantry regiment?"

The group all looked eagerly across the table waiting for the final conclusion; Father Leon obviously enjoying his small lecture.

"I might suggest that he is here on some diplomatic mission as there has not been any mention in the popular press about any interaction between our country and Great Britain. No arms sales nor exchange of military staff – and he would hardly be here if a war had broken out!"

There was some laughter at this extreme hypothesis.

"No gentlemen!" the old priest continued. "I think that our guest is a newly arrived Naval Attaché at the British Embassy here in Quito. As our regiment is the premier one in the city, it would be appropriate that there would have been a suggestion, shall we say, from the government that he is introduced to local military circles via this Mess. No doubt he will be a guest for dinner tonight and we shall probably see more of him now that he is aware that we have gin and tonic. You will need to get some extra supplies in, I think my son." He said with a wink of his eye to the Adjutant.

"A nice, detailed assessment, Padre!" came the reply. "But we shall soon see if it bears some proximity to reality as Enrique has just closed the bar in preparation for dinner and Colonel Ernesto will be here soon. Would anyone wish to make a wager as to the good padre's hypothesis?"

There was no response from the others except a shrug of the shoulders from Xavier who had lost too much in wagers in his own regimental mess over the years and a weak grin from the young José who was still too junior in rank to have any funds left over for wagering.

They got up from their table and walked over to where the other officers of the regiment were now seating themselves at the tables ready for their evening meal. When

Colonel Ernesto arrived everyone stood whilst he, Major Karl and the padre's Englishman, took their seats at the main table. The colonel bade everyone to sit and then asked Padre Leon to say the Grace. This being done, Colonel Ernesto stood and gave a welcome to their guest, introducing him as Capitán de Navío Torrington-Smyth of the Royal Navy, who is newly attached to the British Embassy in Quito.

The Adjutant looked across the table at Father Leon and gave a quick bow of his head; the young José simply sat open-mouth and Xavier smiled, never having any doubt about the padre's assessment of the new arrival. For his part, Father Leon simply sat quietly with his hands together as though in prayer and his eyes were downcast with a look of pious innocence.

Several months now had passed since Father's Leon' demonstration of deductive reasoning. Winter had passed and the warm, dry summer weather had brought some life into Father Leon's little garden. There had also been a change in the daily routine of the regiment. Xavier was well-occupied during the day assisting the ostlers, grooms and other members of the regimental stable in preparation for the departure of the regiment on its annual manoeuvres. There had been some 'sabre rattling' with the Colombia government to the north and so it had been decided by the High Command of the Ecuadoran Army to hold such exercises in the north of the country.

On the appointed day, the Second Regiment of Footguards marched out of its barracks with its band playing a stirring military march and its regimental colours flying proudly. Behind, travelled its baggage train and the horses pulling its three small mountain guns. Xavier, as Master-of-the Horse was not needed on such an expedition as the officers and their grooms were expected to care for the horses and equipment in the field. Xavier was left behind along with Adjutant in command of the remaining staff of the barracks.

This gave Xavier ample spare time to discuss military affairs with the Adjutant and the deeper meanings of God and the church with Father Leon. Xavier now spent considerable time with the old priest, either in the Regimental Chapel where he sometimes assisted with the few family services which were conducted there, or at the father's home at the Jesuit church. The old priest spoke of the work of the Jesuits and of his life within the Society; of his travels in the East, in Asia and of his training in Europe, especially in Rome and in Prussia where the Jesuits had found security after their expulsion in the eighteenth century. Xavier had been especially interested in the old priest's work in the Franciscan mission in the mountains and gladly accepted some tutoring in the language and customs of the people there. He found some comfort in learning Quechua, the language common to parts of Ecuador, Peru and Bolivia because it reminded him of his grandmother's teachings. There were many similarities between that language and her Aymara. Many of the habits of the Andinos of Ecuador were similar to their cousins in Peru.

It was an overcast day, one morning when Xavier sat on the side of his small cot in the Officers' Quarters of the barracks, with a cold, south-easterly wind blowing down off the snows of Volcán Antisana. His spirits were at a low ebb which was not helped with his idleness. The Adjutant had been busy with much of the paperwork of the regiment he therefore, had not been much company, so Xavier sat and looked out of his window at the empty parade ground and the bare walls of the barracks beyond. He had enjoyed his work at the regiment but he knew that it led to nowhere in particular and from his past military experience, he knew that such positions were often transitory depending upon the whims of the current commanding officer and the requirements of the High Command.

One night, sitting on the veranda with Father Leon, he suddenly felt the need to enquire about joining the Jesuits. It was a thought which had been brewing in his mind for several weeks now; the meaning of his existence had become questionable and he felt that there was a need for him to return to a life of fulfilment and duty. Upon reflection of his life over the last few years, he thought that perhaps there may have been some divine guidance in the many turning points of his life; his settled home life, his acceptance into the Military Academy and even his unhappy experience at Huancané and his subsequent resignation of his Commission and flight to Ecuador.

Father Leon had been silent for some time after Xavier had put his question about joining the Jesuits. Then he lifted his gauze and looked directly into Xavier's eyes. "It can be a hard life as well as one of satisfaction, my son. God's work is usually not easy and even His son, Jesus warned his disciples that following Him was fraught with difficulty. There are vows which we take which set us aside from the pleasures and power of earthly society and such are the temptations which are placed in front of us that many men who profess religious piety fail. Do you think that you are strong enough for such a life, my son?"

Xavier looked across the veranda to the garden beyond and the new buds which were beginning to open of the fruit trees. He had thought of emptiness in his life and had felt that perhaps life as a priest may satisfy his desire to bring comfort and spiritual assistance to those around him who may need it. Now he was faced with the difficulties and reality of his belief. The old priest slowly stood up, as the years were now taking their toll, he walked to the edge of the veranda and turned.

"As disciples of Christ, we Jesuits are not often liked, nor our work appreciated, especially by those who think we have too much influence. It has only been a few years now since we have been able to return to this country and the years of exile have weakened the work of the Society. There are still people in high places who mistrust us and try to prevent us from doing our work amongst the common people. You will have to be stronger than perhaps your military training and experience will allow. Are you able to do that and have humility as well?

Xavier looked up and quietly replied "Yes, Father. I think that I will have the strength to do that and a need to follow Christ as well."

The old priest sat down and looked across at his friend. "Well then! If you are resolved to wear the Black Soutane and follow Him then you must know about the path which you will have to take, for it is not an easy one."

Father Leon poured another generous amount of wine into Xavier's chalice and carefully explained what he would have to do to be a Jesuit. "It will take you many years of study, hard work and service before you are even ordained as a Jesuit priest, my son. Are you prepared for that also?" the old priest began.

Xavier simply looked down and nodded his head.

"Well then!" Father Leon continued. "There is usually a long period of discernment in which the individual contemplates his relationship with God and whether or not he is fit for the religious life. This may take years of living alone and thinking about one's own spirituality. However, I know your story, and your past life and believe that you have had extensive time to think about your place in God's world, so I feel that if you say that you are ready to join us, then I would accept that. Besides, the Society has only just re-established itself here in Ecuador and so we cannot afford to waste too much time in long, personal contemplation by men such as yourself. Are you certain that this is what you want?"

Xavier looked up into the old priest's eyes and said with conviction: "Yes, Father. It is."

"I believe that you are sincere in belief, Xavier, so I will see how I can help you. I may be just an old priest sent out to be a military padre, but a long life often means that one also has extensive connections, shall we say, in the organisation of the Society and of the Church in general."

The old priest stood up and went to the wine cupboard from which he took another bottle. "Of course, you will have to start as a Novice which usually takes up to two years of study initially with many more years after that, but if your military education at your academy had the studies in philosophy and other subjects, as I am led to believe by the braggards in this regiment, then this time also may be shortened. However, there will be not skimping in the study of theology and the Spiritual Exercises during this time and at the end you will be required to take our vows of poverty, chastity, and obedience."

"I understand that my new life will require such detailed studies and I am ready for that,

Father. I was a good student at the Academy and not afraid of hard work." Xavier said earnestly now that he could see that there may be some home for him joining the Society and doing something positive with the rest of his life.

"I am glad that you do not mind some hard work, for after this initial period of study, you will be sent out as a Brother or a Scholastic to work for the Society. This might be to one of our churches to assist the priest or to one of our schools or missions to teach. Either way, it will teach you more than you can learn about people than in a Seminary. After that there will a few more years of theology and academic subjects ready for ordination. Do you think that you can last that long?"

"I do." Xavier simply replied.
"Ah!" the old priest laughed. "Well, once that you have become a priest then you can

relax. Yes?" The question was rhetorical and so the old priest continued:

"No! Even ordained Jesuit priests must look forward after a few years of priestly duties before doing what we call our Tertianship— more contemplation and retreats with spiritual exercises to again reflect upon their suitability to do God's work. Only then do you take our final vows including that of obedience to the Pope himself. Only then is your conversion complete and you are suitable to follow the Society's creed —*Ad Maiorem Dei Gloriam*".

Capítulo Ocho:
En la Nueva Sociedad
(Chapter Eight: In New Society)

Father Leon was true to his word. By the end of that very week, he had arranged an interview with the Father Provincial, the head of the Society in Ecuador, who lived in a substantial and beautifully-decorated building not far from the La Iglesia de la Compañía de Jesús. It was obvious to Xavier from the start of the interview that the old priest had spoken very highly of him prior to the meeting. That, and the fact that the Jesuits had but returned to the country a mere seven years before and were looking for suitable new recruits for their company, ensured Xavier's acceptance as a novice.

Xavier was overjoyed with this and felt a great freedom within himself. He had heard of men and women suddenly turning to God but this was no sudden meeting on the road to Damascus; this need had been something which had probably been there since his exodus out of Peru.

Once more he had to go to a regiment's senior officer and explain why he was leaving. Colonel Ernesto heard him out in silence; Xavier had difficulty in explaining his motives for leaving the regiment as talking in terms of religious devotion was new to him. Eventually the Colonel stood up from his desk and walked over to where Xavier was standing. He put his arm around his should and said:

"It takes a man of courage to make such a decision. I have seen men in battle turn to God when they had nowhere else to go. Some men simply knelt and prayed and other looked to the sky and beseeched God in terms both loud and profane. I saw in you, Xavier Aguirre del Río, however a man who was haunted and not at ease with himself and the world. If this call to God is what you want, perhaps even need, then I will give you my best wishes and thoughts for your next journey."

Xavier was heartened by the colonel's words and left the Headquarters with a warm feeling of support. It would be more difficult to explain his departure to his friends in the Officers' Mess. The one-armed Adjutant, Antonio Castillo was a man-of-the-world and simply smiled an enigmatic smile and said with a deep understanding:

"We all walk on the long road to God, my friend. Most of us stumble on our way not knowing where we are going, but you seemed to have lifted your head and see the road clearly before you. Good luck on your journey, vaya con Dios![1]"

---

[1] A common Spanish expression meaning 'Go with God'.

The young Teniente José Ayora found Xavier's decision hard to accept. He had, over the months become his good friend and looked up to Xavier and someone who was always in control and was sure of himself. Becoming a priest was something else as José was not overly religious and had met too many priests who seemed to lack the strength which he saw in his friend Xavier. Never-the-less, he accepted his friend's decision and wished him well.

Once more, Xavier climbed aboard a coach which was to take him on another uncertain journey. It would take him three days to travel to the Jesuit seminary in the town of Cuenca, with most of the trip being on the road which ran along the altiplano of the high Andes southwards from the capital. Both Quito and Cuenca were over 2500 metres above sea level with Quito being the highest at another three hundred metres.

He had feelings of both apprehension and joy as the coach rattled out of Quito and headed south; joy because he now had a purpose and a destination to fulfil it and apprehension about his faith. He made some casual conversation with his fellow passengers, but this time his mind was more occupied with his own thoughts than those of others so he spent most of the time looking out at the passing scenery.

The road for the most part was cobbled; poorly, but far less dusty and rut-filled than the dirt roads he had previously encountered. The countryside was green with many small farms raising cattle and crops. They passed the magnificent, snow-capped cone of the Volcán Cotopaxi far off to their left and then on through the township of Latacunga where the horses were changed and refreshments offered to the passengers. It was late afternoon when the coach finally pulled into the coaching inn of the city of San

Juan de Ambato. Xavier had been proudly informed by Señor Muñoz, one of his fellow travellers and a merchant of the city, that Ambato was known for its production of flowers, fruit, food products, textiles and tanneries. It was also surrounded by several large, snow-capped volcanoes including Cotopaxi, Tungurahua, Carihuairazo, and the largest mountain in Ecuador, Chimborazo. Tungurahua, Señor Muñoz had said, meant 'throat of fire' in the local Quechua language and had been active many times, covering Ambato in a thick layer of grey ash.

The next morning, they continued their journey but without the intercessions of the proud Señor Muñoz. There were only a few people going on to Cuenca and most of those were local people who travelled on the roof. There were few major cities on the next leg of their journey apart from Riobamba where they again changed horses. This city contained many beautiful Spanish colonial buildings, parks and churches. Xavier wished that his stay was longer so that he could explore this beautiful old city.

Instead, he had to reluctantly join the coach the next morning as it continued on its way stopping for the night at a local posada in the small village of Tixan before the steep and winding climb into the hills to Alausi and the city of Cuenca beyond.

It was late that night when the coach stopped at the main square in Cuenca on Calle Benigno Malo. He took his bag which was handed down to him by the old coachman who nodded in the direction of the old church where the coach had stopped.

"This is the Iglesia del Sagrario[2] señor, or as we call it, the 'Old Cathedral'. It dates from the sixteenth century. The came French later,

---

[2] The Church of the Sanctuary.

a long time ago when they were measuring the Earth[3]."

"Thank you, señor. That is most interesting, but can you tell me the way to the Jesuit seminary, please?"

The old coachman turned his head and nodded again to the opposite side of the square where a long, white building stood. "There is the Seminary of San Luis, just across the square." He said as he tossed another bag down to the ground. "As you can see, they are doing some new work on the building. The main entrance is in the middle of building through all of the mud and new bricks. Good luck, señor."

Xavier thanked the coachman and handed up a small coin which was greeted with another nod of the old man's head. Xavier

---

[3] The church's tower was used as a key reference point for the French Geodesic Mission in 1736

took up his small bag, turned and trudged across the large square which had a few cobbled paths leading into its centre. It was poorly lit by several lamps. It was obvious that this too, was undergoing some new work as it was almost bare of grass and other vegetation. He stood for a moment and looked at the long, white building which stood across the wide, cobbled street on the other side of the square.

It had two main storeys with many wide, rounded arches on the ground floor below the tall windows on the floor above. At each end and in the centre, there were towers, each containing a single window to match those below. The central tower had a narrow, gabled roof surmounted by a tall crucifix. The building seemed to be made of stone and bricks and was painted all over in a brilliant white.

There were lights on in the lower, grated windows beyond the arches. A large double wooden door studded with metal stood in the centre archway directly below the upper story with its central tower. At the side of a small postern door Xavier found a small rope which he pulled and heard a bell ringing inside.

The door was opened by an old man dressed in a plain black cassock held up with a wide black belt. He peered out at Xavier over a pair of rimless spectacles and asked him his name. Xavier responded and the old man looked down at a sheath of paper which he produced from a pocket in his cassock.

"Ah! Señor Xavier Aguirre del Río. We have been expecting you." The door was opened and the old man stepped aside for Xavier to enter. He followed the old factotum through a broad archway and into a spacious courtyard, built in the traditional manner with archways on the ground floor and a balconied second floor with many doors leading from it. In front of them was another wide archway which would lead into the inner courtyard.

The old man led Xavier to the stairwell and escorted him up to the far corner of the balcony to one of the many small, wooden doors which opened onto it.

"This is your cell, Brother Xavier." The old man said, opening a door to reveal a small room painted in an austere grey colour and generally devoid of any decoration. On the far wall was a small window below which was a plain wooden table and a chair. There was a crucifix on the wall next to it and apart from the narrow single bed and table, was only a narrow wardrobe as furniture. A small green mat covered part of the stone floor in front of the bed.

"Breakfast is at seven in the refectory near the front gate. Sleep well, brother." With that, the old man closed the door behind Xavier and left him to his thoughts.

He had been slightly taken aback when called 'Brother' Xavier' and now in this small, austere cell, the realised that his new life was not going to be one of freedom nor much comfort. He stripped off his clothes and donned his nightshirt before climbing into bed. Tomorrow would be the first day of his new life.

The cold grey light of dawn was just creeping slowly through his window like some faint grey veil when Xavier awoke the next morning. He reached over and found his pocket watch, being apprehensive that he might have woken too late for the start of breakfast. It was after six but there was plenty of time to dress and go down stairs.

He walked across the bare courtyard paved in brickwork and stone of a simple cross-work pattern. The refectory doors, he had failed to notice the previous evening, opened from the broad archway at the entrance. He entered and found it to be a substantial room with a simple arched ceiling with plain plastered, whitewashed walls. The room was long and narrow with two rows of long tables on each side. It had a long table at the end stretching across the room at right angles to the other tables. He was surprised to find that there were only a few people seated at the tables; he expected a Jesuit seminary to be well-occupied and be a hive of activity. Most of the men in the room wore the black cassock or soutane of the Jesuits which was more of a wrap than a buttoned cassock. A black belt or sash around the waist helped to keep it in place. There was a small group sitting at the head table, most of whom also wore the clerical colour of a Jesuit priest and two who did not. All were older men than most of those who sat at the side tables. These he noticed, mostly wore a simple plain soutane but a few, usually isolated from the rest, wore normal street clothing like himself. Most of the low chatter came those wearing clerical garb; the others sat quietly, looking around the room with some uncertainty. Xavier reasoned that these men were the new intake of which he would be one. He chose a seat at the end of the table next to his fellow civilians, giving a friendly smile to the man who sat several seats from him. There was a tapping of a cup from the head table as one of the priests announced that the Grace would now be said. This complete, a number of servants brought in plates of food, jugs of water and served coffee for those who wished it.

The meal was a simple one; warm bread rolls, various conserves, fruit, water and black, sweet coffee. When most men had finished, one of the head table stood up and lightly tapped his cup for silence. All conversation stopped and everyone looked towards the head table. The man standing was tall and stood very erect. His hair was grey and his face was strong but now graced with a friendly smile.

"Good morning, brothers. For those new to San Luis, allow me to introduce myself as Father Mateo, the Rector of this Seminary. I trust that today will be another beautiful one dedicated to the glory of God. Let us all bow our heads to pray for our work to come."

All bowed their heads in silence as Father Mateo gave the prayer. It was not was long and said in colloquial Spanish without any of the pretensions which Xavier had often heard in some churches. The prayer finished with a short blessing and after the 'Amen', Xavier looked up at Father Mateo whose arms were now outstretched. Father Mateo smiled at the assembled diners and quietly said: "My brothers, please go and prepare for your daily studies and duties, but I would ask our neophytes to remain behind…and perhaps come closer to the front of the room," he said with a slight laugh. "Some of us older men are a little hard of hearing."

Xavier and the other neophytes stood up and moved to the side tables closer to the front of the room whilst the others in clerical garb quietly left. He counted his comrades and noted that there were only six of them. This was also a surprise, as he continued to imagine that there should be a large number of men ready to join the order.

Father Mateo sat down and smiled at the small group of men who now sat before him, uncertain of what formalities would now happen.

"Firstly, my sons. We are all brothers here in the glory of God. You have been chosen to join the Society of Jesus and perhaps one day you may leave this place to do His work. I should tell you that it will not be easy, although I can say that we generally have a good-natured congregation. The other seminarians you will find will be of some help to you. Many men applied for positions here but only you few were chosen. Some found that they were called by their social needs rather than by God and others found that a life of a seminarian would not be to their liking."

Several of Xavier's colleagues looked around as if to see how the others reacted to these comments. Xavier, trained as a soldier continued to look straight ahead at Father Mateo who continued:

"Some of you have chosen to take the longer, more academic pathway as a Scholastic whilst others as Brothers will be equally important and go out to do the work of the

Society in schools, missions and churches.
Let me give you a brief idea of what is ahead
of you."

Father Mateo waited for a moment and then
smiled again before explaining the pathway
of training which they would soon
undertake. His description was both clear
and succinct. He explained that in the First
Studies the Scholastic begins his academic
formation. Depending on his prior education
it will last from two to four years, with a
thorough grounding in philosophy, both
traditional and natural. Here, Father Mateo
stopped briefly as he explained that, as the
order had just been re-established, perhaps
they should call the latter study by its new
name of science. He continued his outline of
their studies by adding mathematics,
history, church administration and some law
to the curriculum. There would be an
introduction to theology, of course, but a
more intense study would come in that

subject at a later stage. Finally, there are what the order called its Spiritual Exercises - a compilation of meditations, prayers, and contemplative practices developed by St. Leon Loyola to help people deepen their relationship with God.

Next, he explained that after a sufficient and successful academic study, the student would then undertake a period of Regency, wherein the scholastic lives and works in a typical Jesuit community. He would be now engaged in full-time in ministry as an Apostolate. This might mean teaching in a secondary school, assisting at a mission or acting as an assistant in a Jesuit church. It may last from two to three years depending upon the student's ability. Here he stopped again and looked carefully at the group of men in front of him:

"Some of you may find the academic life too demanding or stifling. It is at this point, some of you may wish to serve our order as Brothers rather than going on to full ordination as priests Your work would be very valuable and the Society of Jesus depends upon you to take your teachings and the word of God to the common people we serve. Remember that your work is perhaps the most important task of our order, so you may feel becoming a Jesuit Brother is the best path. Those of you who feel that you have been called to the priesthood will find that the road ahead is also not an easy one." He gave a grim smile at this last comment, then continued on with his description of that particular journey.

He explained that after gaining some practical experience, a brother may wish to return to the seminary to study a deeper program of theology and canon law. This could take up to another two years at the end of which candidates for the Catholic priesthood are ordained and take the usual perpetual vows of poverty, chastity and obedience. He then may follow a transitional period as a deacon for six months to a year. Father Mateo looked up again and gave a dramatic sigh and again an enigmatic smile.

"So! You have become a Jesuit priest and now you can retire to some church, mission or school to lead a soft life. No! After ordination and your work as a deacon, you will be assessed, and if suitable may be selected to go on and do further studies – we call it the Tertianship because it is like an extra third year of your neophyte training at the seminary - by revisiting the essentials of Jesuit life and further studies of theology and the history and Constitutions of the Jesuits. There would also be a revisiting of Spiritual Exercises and participation in serving in ministries to the sick, terminally ill or poor. Only then would he solemnly renew his three vows and take the fourth vow, unique to Jesuits, of special obedience to the Pope in matters regarding mission and promising to undertake any mission that the pope may choose".

At the conclusion of this description of their possible future, many of the men with Xavier again looked apprehensive. It seemed a lifetime of study and service, which in fact it was. Father Mateo then introduced the other clerics sitting at the main table, both brothers and priests who would be their teachers and tutors in the years to come.

At the far end of the table, a portly man with a friendly, open face stood up. He had been introduced as Brother Ambrose, who now had the task of matching each neophyte to one of the other clerics who would now explain how each would have their program of study match their past education and experience. Each name was read out and an instructor and an appropriate room number for the interview was given. Xavier was to stay with Father Lorenzo in the Rectory.

Xavier felt somewhat apprehensive in remaining in the long room in which they had just eaten. It was a large room. Its white covered walls and ceiling did little to comfort him, even if there was a fire burning in the large, arched fireplace beyond the head table.

Father Lorenzo came over and sat opposite Xavier at the bare wooden table. He was a gaunt man, of greyish appearance but very black hair. His face showed signs of years of exposure to the weather. Xavier's first impression was that of the grave-diggers which he had often seen in a village after the conclusion of some military skirmish. The smile when it came from Father Lorenzo's thin mouth was brief but friendly. It was his eyes which gave Xavier more encouragement for they were like those of his old friend back in Quito, Father Leon. They were a dark brown but there was a fire in them which he could not explain. When he smiled, they also seemed to glow with an inner strength. Despite the cool exterior, Xavier felt that here was a man who had a strong character forged by much experience and wisdom.

"Well now, Brother Xavier Aguirre del Río what will become of you?" He said with a slight smile as he placed a folio of papers on the table between them. "My old friend and tutor Father Leon Domènech has spoken very highly of you and has sent me a complete file on what you and he have been discussing over this year. I also have comments from Colonel Ernesto whom I also knew many years ago as well as papers and documents from your old regiment and military college in Peru."

Xavier was concerned that so much of his private life was now in the hands of a stranger.

"Oh! I see from your expression that you are concerned about all of this information which we have gathered?" there was another smile and Father Lorenzo looked directly into Xavier's eyes: "We Jesuits are thorough in the research that we do, but do not have any fear, for our enquiries were purely with your best interests in mind. One day you too will be as scrupulous in your enquiries and Father Leon says that you have a remarkable intelligence and insight in deduction. Well, now. We will soon see as I am to be your tutor whilst you are at this seminary. Your education during both your schooldays and at your military academy have been of the best order, I see. Your military experience also will be of some use to you in our order, which as you know was founded by another military man, Saint Ignatius Loyola."

"Thank you, father." Xavier said, now feeling more encouraged. Father Lorenzo continued:

"The Rector and I have discussed the possible pathway which might take here at San Luis and we have conferred with our colleagues who are to be your teachers. Because of your education and experience, there will be some subjects in which you already have some knowledge, so you will probably find yourself attending classes and activities with some of our more senior seminarians. This is common practice and some of them have also had acceleration."

Father Lorenzo stood up and gestured Xavier to do likewise. He walked out of the refectory and into the main courtyard. He swept his arm around in a wide circle then looked directly at Xavier and said: "We have recently reclaimed this, our old seminary and have to re-establish ourselves now that we have returned to South America. No doubt Father Leon told you of our chequered history here in Ecuador. The first Jesuit college here in Cuenca was founded in 1638 by Fathers Francisco de Figueroa and Cristóbal de Acuña, who was its first rector. It remained a seat of learning for almost 130 years until 1767 when we were expelled because we were considered too powerful and interfered too much when governments and the wealthy who often abused the common people. After our restoration in Europe, we returned to Ecuador in 1862, then the college at Cuenca was restored to us."

They walked across the courtyard and through a large archway which was in the far corner. It had several doors on each side and opened out into another, even larger courtyard. This one had trees and plants of many kind. Xavier noticed that there were also several plots of herbs and vegetables growing in the spaces between the cobbled pathways which criss-crossed the garden. Father Mateo opened one of the doors on the side of the archway to reveal a sizeable chapel.

"This is where we have Morning Prayers every day at six, so you will need to get up earlier tomorrow. There are also Evening Prayers at six in the evening and you are expected to attend both, including that of this afternoon. When you return to your cell, you will find that one of the servants would have laid out your new set of clothes, rosary, Bible and other items which our order uses. From now on, you are a seminarian and will be expected to follow our general rules and customs. These are explained in the book provided with the other items. You will receive your schedule of study tomorrow morning after breakfast, as classes usually start at eight promptly each morning. We have a large amount of work in the kitchen and stable should you find keeping to a schedule difficult," Father Mateo said with a smile.

"Thank you, Father. I will do my best." Xavier replied, feeling somewhat like he did when he first entered the military academy.

"Good, Brother Xavier! Then I will see you in the chapel this afternoon. So, for now I suggest that you read what we do here and perhaps familiarize yourself with our other facilities – the well supplied library is upstairs and the ablution rooms are in the far corner of each floor. So, I bid you adieu."

Father Mateo quickly turned and walked back across the outer courtyard towards the main gate, leaving Xavier to return to his cell and to his afternoon reading. Life as a neophyte Jesuit had begun.

Xavier found the daily routine and classes to his liking as he was used to following a disciplined pattern of daily life. On any given day, he would wake up around five in the morning, dress and go to chapel for the Morning Prayers. There was often no fixed routine at chapel but often some leadership from one of the senior seminarians or one of the staff. The session usually involved reading some texts of the Psalms, and meditative contemplation and perhaps a hymn or two this usually took about forty-five minutes.

After chapel, Xavier and the other students went to their rooms or performed their daily ablutions then dressed before breakfast at seven. The meal was usually a simple one with bread, conserves, pastries, fruit and coffee. After breakfast the students went to class with each class lasting about an hour with a generous amount of time to get to the next class or walk about the grounds, if there was some free time, to discuss the content of the lesson or generally socialise with the others.

The vows which Xavier took as a neophyte followed the ancient religious rules of poverty, chastity, and obedience. Nothing he used was owned by him, as all things belonged to the community. Basically, he followed the rules of what it meant to be a Jesuit; love God, love your Jesuit brothers and all people, and love yourself.

When he had no class, he usually occupied his time in reading, researching, and the writing required for his lessons. In the evening, at six p.m., the whole community gathered in the chapel. The students, were often called upon to serve at the mass, read the Scriptures, or give reflections on the scripture of the day. Xavier found that he enjoyed taking his part. After the mass everyone gathered in the library to spend some time together before dinner, chatting about the day and trading stories and jokes.

All the housekeeping chores were divided up among the group and this too, Xavier found to his satisfaction as it meant that he could contribute to the well-being of his colleagues. There was a good balance of work and relaxation, with an attitude of serving rather than being served soon developing.

At the end of the day, he prayed the Examen, which was a method the Jesuits used to review the day's events and to understand the flow of one's own emotions and habits. He was thus taught to believe that every event, every feeling that he experienced during the day, was a way of God communicating to him. In himself, Xavier was happy. He had found a purpose in life. The life of a student priest and the routine was not much different from his early days in the Military Academy. Above all, his new studies gave him a better insight to his inner self and of the world around him. In addition, he found that, being older than most of his fellow students, he was popular with most and was respected. He made several good friends and he looked forward to his future. He had stopped running.

Capítulo Nueve:
El Cáliz Dorado
(Chapter Nine: The Golden Chalice)

It was in Xavier's second year at the seminary of San Luis when an event occurred which shocked most of the good people of Cuenca.

As part of its social commitment to the local community, the seminary had a day in which relatives and guests could visit its main buildings and mix socially for a short time with the students. It was a good time for local and some distant people to visit their relatives and to see how the seminary operated.

This was a happy day for many, except for Xavier who had only written contact with his sister, Gabriella and on some rare occasions with his younger brother, Alejandro.

He had made several close friends at the seminary however in Juan Ortega and Carlos Jiménez.

Ortega was the son of a merchant from Quito and had always wanted to be a priest. His family was wealthy and traced their ancestry back to some of the early Spanish settlers in Ecuador. Tall and slender, there was something of the ascetic about him and Xavier liked his thoughtfulness and learning.

Jiménez was a total contrast to his friend and came from a small village near Ambato which was some two hundred kilometres north of Cuenca. He was of the Salasaca people and hoped to return to the Ambato district and serve there as a priest. Being of a quick intelligence, he had received some patronage from his Parish and from some wealthy merchants in Ambato who wished promote the welfare of the local people. He was a cheerful fellow, typical of many

Andinos who always a good story to tell and at home would always have a jar of freshly brewed Chica[1] on hand.

There was another seminarian with who Xavier sometimes shared some time; mainly in study or deep and often aggravated discussion about some theological point of view. Rodrigo Navarro Torres was friendly enough with Xavier but did not socialise with most of the other seminarians, especially Xavier's other two close friends. He kept mostly to himself but often sought Xavier's opinion on intellectual matters. Xavier felt sorry for this young man feeling that he was a troubled soul and would probably not survive the rigors of his studies. For his part, Navarro expressed confidence in his future but spent much of his contact with Xavier talking about his wealthy and noble family in Guayaquil who were

---

[1] A corn beer brewed at home and commonly found in many communities in the Andes.

descended from one of the first Conquistadores to come to Ecuador. Xavier, at times felt the need to council him when he expressed a low opinion of the local people; hardly that of a future Jesuit priest.

Now in the chapel, there were several chalices sitting on a silver tray on the altar. Most of them were of simple earthenware and had been made by several of the Andino peoples who lived within the Cuenca region and bore many of the traditional symbols of those people. One. However, was of gold. This had been donated by a wealthy family, the Clemente family, and was reputed to have been of Incan origin, looted from some palace centuries ago. The chalices were used for various feast days as part of the Sacrament, the golden chalice being reserved for Christmas and Easter services.

After the seminary had opened its doors to visitors, the golden chalice was found to be missing. The discovery was made when the chapel was being cleaned and readied for the evening devotions.

Immediately the rector was notified and a thorough search was made by the priests and brothers of the teaching staff. When the chalice was not found in the chapel nor the sacristy, there had been no alternative but to search the rest of the seminary, including the cells of its students. Nothing was found and so the local Prefecture was called in to make a more thorough search and to make enquires about the city. The news soon spread rapidly through the area and everyone was dismayed that such a theft could occur within a seminary.

Xavier was, like the other seminarians, dismayed too, but decided to look into the matter himself. There were no obvious suspects so he had to make some general observations and his own private search of the common areas of each building.

On the evening of the second day, Xavier was sitting in a quiet corner of the seminary library when Rodrigo Navarro sat down next to him. The young man seemed agitated and asked Xavier if he had heard of any news from the prefecture about the missing chalice.

"No, not yet," said Xavier in a casual tone.

"There were too many visitors here the other day. Especially some of the local people. Andinos are simple people, poor to boot. A golden chalice like that would set them and their families up for life."

Xavier was rather shocked and dismayed at this comment, not only because of his own ancestry but because he knew that such common and brazen thieving was not in the usual character of the people of the Andes. He looked across at Navarro and told him so. The young man did not like to be reproached and so he stood up, stared at Xavier for a short moment and then stormed out of the library. Xavier felt that such a comment and the young man's attitude was worth further investigation.

Xavier did not suspect any of the recent visitors to the seminary, as few had visited the chapel alone; mostly coming in with their relatives or other seminarians. On that day, there had always been a seminarian in the chapel to explain to the visitors the various paintings and artefacts which were contained within it, including the tray of chalices. He himself had been given such a task during the morning and his friends had also shared in this responsibility. The chalice must have been taken late in the afternoon when most of the guests had departed.

Xavier made his general search of the chapel, library, common rooms and hallways of the seminary in as a discrete manner as possible. He observed his fellow students just as discretely, but without any obvious evidence coming to hand.

In his cell he sat and thought about the events of the previous days. Back at the regiment in Quito, Father Leon had taught him a way to recall the small details which were often ignored during such a general investigation. He sat on his bed, closed his eyes and relaxed his body by imagining his muscles as being twisted rope. From the toes upward, he imagined these ropes slowly untwisting until those of his neck and face were once more limp strands. Then he put all of his daily thoughts out of his mind by slowly repeating in his mind the first part of the 'Hail Mary':

"Ave Maria, gratia plena, Dominus tecum".[2]

Then he would recall the past events which came to him as a vision. He saw the visitors arriving through the open gates of the seminary and meeting their friends and loved ones in the outer courtyard which had been decorated with garlands of flowers, flags and holy banners. There were tables of food and drink and the guests were talking to their sponsors. He saw his friends Carlos and Juan laughing together and sharing drinks with their invited friends; he saw Rodrigo Navarro in animated conversation with a beautiful girl. Stop! This was very unusual for Navarro to show much emotion to anyone, and especially to a young woman. He had often decried the value of women

---

[2] In full in Latin, this is: *"Ave Maria, gratia plena, Dominus tecum. Benedicta tu in mulieribus, et benedictus fructus ventris tui, Iesus. Sancta Maria, Mater Dei, ora pro nobis peccatoribus, nunc et in hora mortis nostrae. Amen"*. Or in English: *"Hail Mary, full of grace, the Lord is with Thee. Blessed art Thou amongst women, and blessed is the Fruit of thy womb, Jesus. Holy Mary, Mother of God, pray for us sinners now and at the hour of our death. Amen"*.

and now he was laughing and freely speaking with this beautiful young girl.

Xavier concentrated and let his mind gather its thoughts about the incongruous couple. The girl was obviously younger than Navarro. There were some similarities in her stance and mannerisms but she was not of European descent but rather had the lovely completion, black hair and high cheekbones of an Andino girl. His sister perhaps?

Then in his mind Xavier saw the girl offer Navarro a goblet of wine. He deliberately poured a little onto the ground and then drank from it. This was a custom well-known to Xavier. It was considered to be good manners within Andino society to offer a small amount of food and drink to Pachamama, the ancient Incan goddess of the Earth and protector of children.

Then Xavier's mind wandered, still thinking about Rodrigo Navarro. There was something else about him which Xavier had observed briefly and passed over without moments thought. What was it? Yes, he remembered now! There was Navarro sitting opposite him at the evening meal not long after the robbery. He reached across to take some bread from the central bowl and whilst his hands had been scrubbed clean, there were slight traces of brown clay beneath his fingernails, evidence that he had been working in the pottery section of the seminary's recreation room.

Xavier suddenly opened his eyes and sat bolt upright. He now knew where the golden chalice had been taken and why it had not been found even after a thorough search of every room in the seminary. He got up and rushed out of his cell and along the balcony in search of brother Rodrigo. He knocked at his cell door and there was no answer so he went to the library where most of his fellow students would be at this time of day, reading or discussing some aspects of their previous lessons. He was not there also.

Downstairs, Xavier looked into many of the small recesses and in the garden of the inner courtyard where students often went for solitude. Nothing.

Walking through the archway which connected the two courtyards, Xavier saw that the chapel door was open. He went in and in its dim light, lit only by a small lamp at the altar, he saw a lone figure at prayer in one of the forward pews. It was Navarro.

Xavier entered and quietly walked down the aisle and when he was a few paces from where Navarro was praying, he softly spoke a common saying in Quechua, the language of the Incas and still that of many Andino peoples:

"Diosman wititaqa puëdentsik, pëta kuyaqkunawan amigo karmi"³.

Without thinking, Navarro instinctively replied with the usual affirmation to this saying in the same language:

"Llapämi kuyanakuyä"⁴.

Suddenly realising what he had said, Navarro looked up in fright as Xavier knelt down beside him and put one arm around his shoulders and quietly said:

"Your cross is too heavy to bear alone, Brother Rodrigo. I know about the chalice and wish to help you. Come! Let us go back to your cell as I believe that all of the answers are to be had there.

---

³ Translated from the Quechua: "You can come near to God if you make friends with people who love God"
⁴ Translated from the Quechua: "And what good friends we've come to be!"

Navarro looked at Xavier and he had tears in his eyes; his head now slumped down onto his chest and he slowly stood up. The two men walked slowly out of the chapel; Xavier's arm still around the other man's shoulders. At the door, Xavier took his arm away and the two seminarians walked together up the stairs and to Navarro's cell.

They went in and Navarro sat on his bead, his eyes downcast and his hands nervously clasping together in his lap.

As he suspected, there was an earthenware chalice containing a variety of pens sitting on the desk below the window. It had been crudely fashioned and some of the decoration was incomplete. It had been made in a hurry.

Xavier went over and picked it up. It was much too heavy for a simple earthenware chalice, so he tipped out the pens and began to lightly tap the chalice on the side of the desk much like one would lightly tap the shell of a hard-boiled egg on the side of a pot. Small cracks appeared in the earthenware and Xavier used his finger and thumb to peel off the hardened flacks of the pottery shell. The bright flash of gold shone in the sunlight streaming through the window. The golden chalice had been found!

Xavier completed his task and swept the broken pieces of pottery into the pocket of his soutane. He turned to Navarro and stretched out his hand which was holding the chalice.

"It is now your task, Brother Rodrigo to undo the wrong which you have done. God is merciful and you will be forgiven, but only you can return this chalice whilst the chapel is empty".

Navarro took the chalice and looked up at Xavier: How did you know it was me?" he asked in a faint voice.

Xavier sat down on the bed next to his friend and quietly revealed how he had come to the conclusion as to who was the thief and where he had taken the chalice.

"Firstly, you have been much too vocal about the nobility of your family and the lack of worth of the local people. Secondly, I suspected that you were not what you claimed and this was confirmed when I saw you talking to that beautiful girl when our guests were here. Is she your sister?"

"My half-sister." Navarro replied.

"Next, there was the offering to Pachamama. Only one who respects the customs of the Andino would have done such a thing. You are a mestizo – of mixed Spanish and local blood, I assume?"

"Yes." Navarro replied. Xavier noticed that now he sat more upright and looked more relaxed. He continued.

"Yes, Brother Xavier. I stole the chalice as it was a symbol to me of an oppressive time in our country's history; a time when the Spaniards, represented by my family, oppressed the common people. I am indeed the son of Hector Navarro Torres, descendent of proud Conquistadores, but also the offspring of one of his servants, my mother Maria. She was cast out of the Navarro household and when I was born, I was raised by my mother in her village of Llacao which is not far from here. The young woman that you saw was indeed my younger sister, Luciana. My father did, however have some feelings of guilt towards my mother, so he sent money for my upbringing and education. Luckily, I was a good scholar and had also served in the local church where Father Sebastián gave me more encouragement to serve God. With my father's influence and the good Father's recommendation, I secured a position here at the seminary. Can you understand what torment I have had in my life, Xavier?

"Yes, my friend. I too am a mestizo and have had some difficulty in my family also, and now, like yourself seek to be of some service to God. Come, it is time for you to return the chalice. I will come with you as far as the chapel to see that it is unoccupied. Then I will leave you to do what is right and to your own conscience about what you make of your future."

The two men returned to the chapel doors. Xavier quickly looked in and motioned Navarro to enter. He then closed the door and returned to his own cell, confident that his friend would find repentance.

It was to everyone's surprise that the golden chalice had returned to its place of honour; everyone except Xavier and Navarro. A prayer was said for its return and forgiveness for the one who had taken it.

A week later, Rodrigo Navarro Torres quietly left the seminary. The night before, he had quietly come to Xavier's cell and thanked him for his help in regaining his peace and his soul. Then he left.

It was after the morning prayers the next day when Father Lorenzo caught up to Xavier as he walked back to his cell to prepare for breakfast.

"Thank you, Xavier for what you did for Brother Rodrigo and San Luis. The Rector told me of his confession and your part in the return of the golden chalice. That was certainly a very interesting piece of deductive reasoning which went beyond the investigative powers of the rest of us – and the local prefecture, I must add."

"Brother Rodrigo needed help and I was able to give it. That's all, Father." Xavier said quietly. "What will become of him?"

Father Lorenzo looked at him and smiled:

"What are the three moral virtues of the Inca? Ama Sua; Ama Llulla; and Ama Quella are they not?[5]"

Xavier looked at his mentor with some surprise.

"Our Brother Rodrigo," he continued, "will go back to his village with a simple letter

---

[5] From the Quechua: "do not be a thief; do not be a liar and do not be idle."

from the rector that the life of a Jesuit was not suited for him with a recommendation that he follow the path of another order which has fewer demands. Nothing more will be said of it here. Do you agree, Brother Xavier?"

Xavier smiled and quietly said, "Thank you Father Lorenzo, that is for the best for I truly believe that Rodrigo Navarro is now a better man and the story of the missing golden chalice is now at an end. Amen"

Capítulo Diez:
La Nueva Misión
(Chapter Ten: The New Mission)

Time passed quickly for Xavier at the Seminary San Luis and he was now entering his third year as a student Scholastic. It was now the time for him to enter his Regency when he would go out and live in a Jesuit community for two years.

He had been appointed as an assistant to the Jesuit College in Riobamba which was a good days' journey to the north. Here he was to assist in the teaching of Natural Philosophy, a subject for which he had shown a particular talent in his studies at San Luis.

The College of San Pedro had been founded by the Jesuits in the 1830's and had a good reputation. Its students were mostly the sons of the wealthy classes of the city, but there had been a recent outreach for those of outlying areas who wished their sons to have a good education. These students were few in number as traditionally, young boys in the country worked with their families on the many farms and in the small villages nearby. Xavier found the Jesuit community, which served the school and the local parish, to be friendly and hard working. He learnt a lot about the daily working routine and tasks of a Jesuit Brother and he also often assisted the priests in services at the local Jesuit church.

Teaching was something new to him and he found that he interacted well with the students. The college routine was an intensive one and he had several classes of different age groups to teach. The students, he found were usually of good character and attentive in class but there were the occasional few who were restless and often tried his patience.

The curriculum of Natural Philosophy gave him a wide spread of new and interesting subject matter to study. Biology, chemistry, physics, mathematics and the new subject of geology, were all of great interest to study and prepare for his classes and his teaching style was often very popular with his students.

Naturally, he had a junior position in the college as an Apostolate, but the older brothers and Father Pablo, the Principal were happy to have someone who knew a little about Natural Philosophy, as such teachers were hard to come by. Xavier was also expected to assist in the general running of the college, including their sporting, cultural and religious activities and after a few months, he soon found that the pattern of daily life was not as arduous as he first thought. However, he did have many reservations about making teaching his final profession as he sometimes found that his restless nature and independence of spirit did not often suit the confines of an educational institution and its regular routine.

It was in the last month of his first year in Regency and the students had left the college for their summer holidays. Xavier was sitting in the staff common room reading a local newspaper when Father Pablo, the principal sat down in the chair by his side. Father Pablo seemed to have the ability to appear suddenly, much to the chagrin of students, especially those who were up to no good. He looked down at Xavier who put his paper down.

"Brother Xavier", Father Pablo said with some concern written across his face, "I have just received a letter in the morning mail which requests changing the location of your Regency appointment"

Xavier was perplexed and put his newspaper down. Why was he to be given a new location to complete his Regency? – It was highly unusual. He looked at Father Pablo and saw that he too was perplexed. Father Pablo continued:

"What is more concerning, Brother Xavier, is that this letter comes from the Father Provincial himself in Quito. It simply asks us to relinquish your post here at the College and advise you that the location for your second year of regency has changed and that a coach will arrive on the morning of the 16th to take you to your new post. That is tomorrow! Do you know anything about this, Brother Xavier?"

Xavier took the letter that was offered to him, read it and handed it back to the principal. "Why no! Father Pablo. I am just as shocked as you are to hear this! I cannot think as to why my duty to the order is being changed.

I have heard no complaints about my teaching and my students and their parents seem to be happy with my work. I have been very happy here."

"No, no, no." said Father Pablo. "Your work here has been most exemplary. There have been no complaints; you would have heard it directly from me long before this. No. This is a higher matter. The Father Provincial would not be involved unless it was not of the highest importance."

The Principal stood up and tucked the letter into the pocket of his soutane. "Well, it is beyond us, my friend. We will just have to go on the road that God has chosen for us. Omnes viae eius viae Deum sequi fimus,[1]" he said in Latin. He made the sign of the cross and left Xavier to his thoughts.

Xavier sat for a moment but without any thoughts. He could not understand why his

---

[1] "It is the destiny of us all to follow our chosen road to God."

Regency had been changed. Why? The good father was right. There was nothing for him to do but trust in God and pack his few belongings to leave the college. That evening, he said goodbye to his friends who had heard the news from the college secretary – schools hold no secrets.

The next morning, after breakfast, Xavier once more said his farewells to the few friends who had gathered around him as he walked out of the main door of Clergy House attached to the college and down the long, cobbled road leading to the main gate to await the arrival of his coach.

It was going to be a nice day in Riobamba as the sky was clear except for a few wispy clouds and there already were several people out walking through the broad park across the street. There was a slight breeze blowing from the east which brought a little chill from the snows of Volcán Chimborazo and rustled the fronds of the palms which ringed the park.

It was well over an hour before a coach pulled up on the opposite side of the road. Xavier took up his small bag and walked across to it. There was an indifferent salute from the coachman who climbed down to take his bag and put it up into the storage compartment on top of the coach. Xavier thanked him and, opening the coach door climbed in.

He was surprised to find that coach was already occupied. There was a broad-chested man in the military uniform of the Ecuadorian Army already sitting in the coach. He looked across at Xavier and gave him that familiar enigmatic smile.

"Colonel Ernesto!" Xavier exclaimed, recognising his old friend and Commanding Officer of the 2nd Guards Regiment.

"The same, Xavier – or should I say Brother Xavier? It is good to see you again."

Xavier was now even more perplexed than before. Why would his new posting concern a high-ranking army officer? Then he noticed something different about his old friend. "You have been promoted! A full Colonel, no less! But tell me, what is this all about?"

The coach started off with a sudden rattling of harness. Colonel Ernesto learned forward and said: "Yes, as you have rightly observed, I am indeed now a full colonel and am now head of what you might call our 'information' bureau."

"'Military Intelligence', you mean." Xavier said with a smile.

Colonel Ernesto leant back and laughed. "Well, I had forgotten that you were once in the military yourself and that Father Leon had taught you more about intelligence gathering than many of my young officers. So, I am reassured that I have found the right man. You see, we have a problem. By 'we', I mean the governments in Quito and Lima."

Xavier was now intrigued that the government of Peru may now be involved in an Ecuadorian problem. The Colonel continued:

"I am sure that you are aware, that occasionally there are minor border disputes between Ecuador and Peru because the Spaniards were very vague when they came to drawing borders between their new colonies. The Liberators who then freed these colonies from their Spanish masters were also often uncertain about borders and often hotly debated where they should be. This is still part of our political reality and so units of the military of both Ecuador and Peru are bound to meet somewhere, usually in our Amazonian provinces, either by chance or by design. These sudden encounters are mostly brief affairs with a few shots in the air and words of derision, but more recently there was an encounter which could have grave political ramifications to both countries."

Colonel Ernesto looked out of the window at the passing houses as the coach continued north on the road to Ambato. He continued his story:

"Unfortunately, this time our army reconnaissance unit, under an over-zealous officer, advanced well into Peruvian territory. There was a sharp exchange of fire with the Peruvians, but several of our men were captured before our unit could withdrew. So here is the problem: the Peruvian Army now have three of our soldiers in a secure camp in the jungle just across the border. The area is very remote and the only way which we can access it is by travelling down the Río Pastaza. There is a road, poor to be sure, but a road never-the-less, which goes part of the way from the city of Baños de Agua Santa. Do you know of it?"

Xavier sat back and thought for a moment. "Yes, I have heard of it but I have never travelled there. Is it not a place of religious pilgrimage?"

"Yes, that is true. They say that the Virgin appeared in a waterfall there and its waters cure the sick. Then later She saved the people from Volcán Tungurahua, on which slopes the city is built, by diverting water onto the lava which threatened the city. People from all over Ecuador and even beyond, go there for a cure in the hot springs. The Dominicans had much to do with its foundation, so you will have to complete part of your studies with them. Your Father Provincial is a particular friend of mine and Father Mateo at the seminary has, on his request, approved of this change. The Dominicans have been asked for their support and you are to be temporarily enrolled in their order at Baños."

"Thank you, Colonel, but why have you asked for my help. I am just a lowly Jesuit brother – not even a priest?"

Colonel Ernesto again leaned over close to Xavier's face and said: "Yes, Xavier but you are also someone whom I can trust – a man of many talents. You are also a former army officer. Father Leon had told me that you understand the indigenous people and speak fluent Quechua. Where we are going, that will be a great advantage as there was once a small Jesuit mission near there before your order was expelled from the country. As well, you are a Peruvian by birth and trusted by me. Of course, being a man of the Church and dressed in a black soutane will greatly help with first impressions. Do you see that?"

Xavier thought for a moment, slightly embarrassed at such compliments. "Yes." He replied. "I can see some military strategy in your reasoning and of course I will help you. Governments can look after themselves."

"Good!" Colonel Ernesto replied. "Our new President, Gabriel García Moreno is a reformer and is keen to have this matter resolved with the utmost urgency and as quietly as possible, you understand?"

"That is to be sure," replied Xavier. "There is too much for both our countries to lose. Perhaps a priest – albeit only a student priest – would be most beneficial and the protection of the local people is one of the ideals of our order. So! On to Baños, then!"

Baños was only about eighty kilometres away on roads which were reasonable for the mountains, explained the colonel. The city had been built in the narrow valley which follows the course of the Río Pastaza on its way to the Río Marañon and then on to the mighty Amazon. It is also on the slopes of Volcán Tungurahua which in the Quechua language means 'Throat of Fire.' This also provides the rich, hot mineral springs for which the city is noted. Now Tungurahua is an active volcano which regularly spews out a cloud of ash which covers the city. This is taken for granted by the local people who call the mountain 'Mama Tungurahua' and pray both to the Virgin and to Pachamama, the old Incan goddess of the Earth for their protection from the mountain.

The coach made a brief stop at Ambato to change horses for the next leg of our journey east through the hills to Baños. During our brief stop for refreshment, Colonel Ernesto retired to the bathroom at the coaching posada and changed out of his military uniform and into a more sombre set of civilian attire. Now he looked like any prosperous merchant travelling on business. Finally, the coach crossed over the small bridge over the Río Bascún, which trickles its way down through the rocks off the slopes of the volcano and into the Río Pastaza, then into the city of Baños de Agua Santa or the Baths of Holy Water.

It was coming onto a cold night as the coach pull up outside of the Priory of the Dominicans in the city's centre. They were greeted at the gate by two of the Dominican friars wearing their traditional black cappa or cloak over their white habits. The older man had that superior look of one who can lead men and his habit was clean and well fitted. There was a large cross hanging down his front and Xavier suspected that he was the prior.

"Welcome to our poor Priory of Nuestra Señora del Rosario[2]" said the older man as he came up to the door of the coach. He was indeed the prior here and he introduced himself as Fray Albert.

"Our Provincial Prior in Quito sent urgent word that we should give you all the assistance that is available to us and that it should be done with the utmost discretion. My brother here..." he said turning to the other friar "...is Fray Dominic, my most trusted assistant. He will show your driver the way to one of our empty Charity Houses which we have prepared for your use. I hope that we will meet soon in more sociable circumstances."

"Thank you, Fray Albert. Yes, we will meet soon, I trust. Goodnight." Colonel Ernesto said, putting his arm through the open window to shake the prior's hand. The other

---

[2] "Our Lady of the Rosary

friar climbed up with the driver and the coach quietly moved off through the darkened streets of the city. They rounded the small square which stood in front of the priory and church where a few people were hurrying home down a long street which led to the riverside. Here they turned into a side lane which seemed to run along the river bank itself with only a few small, walled houses stifling the sounds of the gurgling waters beyond.

Eventually they stopped at a two-story building which did not have the perimeter walls and gates of the other houses in the lane, but was open at the front where two small lamps illuminated double wooden doors. There were lights on inside the house and at the sound of the coach coming to a stop, one of the doors opened and another friar in his white habit came out to open the door of the coach.

"Welcome to our Charity House. I am Fray Gabriel and I and my brother Fray Sebastian are at your service." He said with a slight bow.

Colonel Ernesto and Xavier got out of the coach and followed Fray Gabriel into the house. The coachman had thrown down their two small bags from the roof of the coach where they were expertly caught by the burley Fray Dominic.

Inside, the house was well furnished with a small fire burning in a large fireplace over on the side of the room. There was food on a long wooden table where Fray Sebastian was standing at the end ready to serve. Both men were young and seemed to be pleased to greet their guests. Xavier and Ernesto sat down in the chairs which were now pulled out for them to sit as wine was poured into the goblets placed in front of them.

Fray Dominic entered the room carrying the bags. It was the first time that Xavier had to examine this friar and saw that he differed in many respects from the two men who now waited at their table.

Fray Dominic was past middle age with the typical stocky build of an Andino. His chest was broad and he was shorter than his two colleagues. His now mostly grey hair topped a face that showed the signs of a hard life. Xavier thought that his broad nose had been broken at some stage, for it did not seemed to fit evenly in his leathery brown face. It was only his eyes which showed the man inside. They were deep brown, like some dark pool at night which seemed to sparkle in the firelight of the room.

"I will put your bags upstairs in your rooms, Señores. They are at the top of the stairs and the bathroom is at the end of the corridor. I will see you in the morning."

With that, he trudged up the bare stairway with the two bags. Xavier turned his attention to the food which had been placed before him; a generous plate of arroz con pollo[3].

After dinner, Xavier retired to his room whilst Colonel Ernesto chatted with the two friars and quickly inspected the lower floors of the house. It was built of adobe bricks but, like many of the houses in Baños it had been thoroughly plastered and then painted in a pastel colour; this house had been painted in a light green. He walked outside to inspect the grounds but there was very little to see in the dark. The house sat at the end of the long lane of houses with walls and wide gates but this house took up most of the block so that there was very little access around to the rear of it. When he did manage to grope his way around one side of the house on a narrow

---

[3] Arroz con pollo: is a delicious Ecuadorian dish of chicken and rice cooked with onions, tomatoes, peppers, celery, garlic, achiote, cumin, cilantro, among other ingredients.

strip of rough pebbles which came to a sudden end, he found that the house had been built right up to the river bank with a substantial drop down to the river below. From his military point of view, the house seemed very secure as it was unlikely that anyone could approach from the river and the rest of the house seemed sturdy enough with barred windows and two strong, wooden doors. Satisfied, he went back inside and wishing the two friars a 'good night' went upstairs to bed.

Xavier had found the room with his small bag resting against the door and went in. There was a candle burning on a small table near a large bed which had a thick and colourful bedspread. There was a highly polished wardrobe with a dressing table, a comfortable-looking armchair and a brightly woven mat on the polished wooden floor. There was another door on the opposite wall that he opened and went through. It opened out onto a short balcony with low walls of unplastered adobe, a wooden roof above. A large woven hammock stretched across most of its length. The sound of the Río Pastaza was loud as it splashed its way around the large boulders which filled most of its course. The moon had come out, its light sparked on the splashes of water below. Xavier turned and went inside, closing the door behind him. The sound of the river was softer now and he would sleep well to its happy sound.

The next morning, Xavier woke with a start and found the early morning light just beginning to fill the room. He arose and put on his coat as the morning was still cold. He went outside onto the balcony and found that he could look down the long, steep-sided valley of the Río Pastaza. The sun was just coming up over one of the spurs of the hills to his right. He could now make out the opposite bank of the river through a large bushy tree which had grown up from the floor of the valley deep below. The river bed was completely full of larger bounders around which the stream had to flow. The bank on the opposite side was vertical but ended in a flat terrace upon which were several houses. The entire bank on the opposite side was totally covered in bushes and trees giving a luxurious green vista down the valley which seemed to narrow in the distance.

Xavier stretched out on the hammock which occupied most of the balcony. It was made of a very strong cotton cloth, beautifully woven in intricate stripes, similar to the designs he had seen in the villages of his own Peru. He lay there thinking of what the future may hold when a slight movement in the tree near the balcony caught his eye. It was a very small bird hovering almost stationary at a large flower. It had an iridescent green body with a white breast, black wing tips and a dark blue head. He watched as it flitted from flower to flower of the tall tree which grew near the balcony. It was a most magnificent sight to start the day.

True to his word, Fray Dominic arrived very early in the morning, before breakfast to which he invited himself, and sat down at the table with Xavier and Colonel Ernesto. "It is a great day for a long journey, my friends!" he said with a broad smile on his leathery brown face and a sparkle in his eyes. "You will want for nothing as our good prior has provide food, drink and shelter for our wandering. They are on my small cart outside, along with my good little mule Conchita. She is a gentle friend but unused to being harnessed, you understand. So, we should be on our way as soon as you both can manage."

Turning to the two friars working in the kitchen, he called out:

"Brother, may I have an egg with my rolls and coffee, please?"

He turned back to Xavier and Colonel Ernesto: "They are good men, those two. They work hard at the priory and for our guests as you have found, for we are the Order of Preachers and they do good work here. But for myself, I prefer to get out and tend to my children who live here in my mountains and sometimes down to where we are going in the 'Green Hell' as it is called. My two brothers here would not be comfortable there; they are more domestics than Dominicans!"

He gave a short laugh at his little play on words, then set to with his egg which Fray Gabriel had placed before him. Xavier and Colonel Ernesto finished their breakfast and thanked the two friars for their attention, then went to their rooms to get ready for their trip.

Colonel Ernesto had changed into his army fatigues; baggy navy-blue trousers, grey tunic, high black boots and his kepi which matched his trousers. It was still a little chilled so he also wore a dark grey cloak which also served to hide his uniform from prying eyes. Xavier had been asked by Colonel Ernesto to wear his soutane as proof of his vocation, but he supplemented his clothing with a heavy coat, a good pair of boots and his broad-brimmed black hat. They were ready to go on their new mission. Outside, Fray Dominic was waiting by the side of his mule who stood patiently with an occasional flicking of her ears and a swish of her tail.

"This is my Conchita!" Fray Dominic said with some pride, clapping a hand on the mule's back. "I have called all of my mules, Conchita over the many years I have wandered these mountains. The original was the mother of a girl I once knew. She was not as docile nor friendly as my Conchita, but that is another story," he laughed. "So come, now. Climb aboard. Conchita can take us for part of the way for the road to the east later will change to a mere track and then to an overgrown path through the jungle. My full name is Fray Dominic Vargas Mendoza but that is much too formal and too much for the mouth. All of my flock and those who know me better call me Brother Dom and you should do the same if you please."

The road was quite respectable, being cobbled whilst in the city limits but then it became dirt and dusty where it was called 'El Camino Real' or the 'Royal Road' because this was the route that the Inca would take on their way to the eastern part of their empire, Antisuyu[4]. After a few kilometres, they passed a large hacienda, or homestead, which was now deserted and in great need

____

[4] Quechua *anti* east, *suyu* quadrant – the eastern part of the Inca Empire which bordered on the modern-day Upper Amazon region.

of repair as one of its large double wooden doors now hung at some obscene angle on its broken hinges. It had very high walls of stone and adobe with some high barred windows and was built at a time when the early Spanish colonialists needed to defend their property against the local people whose land they had taken.

"That is the Hacienda San Rafael" said Brother Dom, pointing across to the building with its hanging door. It was built in the late eighteenth century by a Spanish nobleman Don Gervasio de León, who saw that this region would control much of the trade going from the wealth of the Amazon Basin to Quito. He was only moderately successful, however and his fortunes waned, but the hacienda stayed in his family. Then following our independence there had been several owners but the estate generally fell into disrepair."

Colonel Ernesto studied the old building as they passed, noting that perhaps old Don Gervasio was right that it would be a strategic place between Quito and the new provinces in the Amazon Basin. He would keep that as future reference as a possible supply depot.

The road then became more rocky but still wide and relatively flat for a mountain road. It ran along the southern side of the river, mostly away from its unstable banks but occasionally, there would be a view of the wild Río Pastaza as it churned and gurgled its way around the large boulders which made up its bed. Brother Dom commented that now this road was generally called the 'Vía a Baños' or the 'Way to Baños'. He joked that outsiders coming up from the east and new to the area also took the rather literal Spanish meaning for it as the 'Way to the Bathroom' as 'bath' was the other translation of the city's name. Going east in the opposite direction, the route was also called the 'Gateway to the Amazon' for it was to that vast river basin that they were now headed. The road continued to wind its way around the steep ridges of the high, green hills that had been formed by the fast-flowing Río Pastaza. They crossed a large wooden and stone bridge over to the other side of the river and continued on tier way; the road and the always going downhill.

Conchita kept up a slow and steady pace allowing the three men to talk of many things. They soon found out that they had many things in common; all three had been soldiers. Xavier suspected that their host, Brother Dom was a restless soul who preferred the outdoor life rather than the confines of a priory or town. His general way of speaking, his good humour and activity as well as his weather-beaten appearance, suggested that in a time past, he may have been put him in 'harm's way' as the expression goes. Brother Dom had been reluctant to talk much about his past but much about the present and future. He finally confessed that as a very young student, he had been caught up in the revolutionary fervour at that time and had become a volunteer in the Yaguachi Battalion of the Army of General Antonio José de Sucre, and had fought in the bloody battle of Pichincha.[5]

The road was unexpectedly short and within a few hours, the narrow, steep-sided valleys began to open out and the river began to widen and slow it its pace down towards the Amazon Basin. The temperature of the air and its humidity had also become

---

[5] The Battle of Pichincha took place on 24 May 1822, on the slopes of the Pichincha volcano, 3,500 meters above sea-level, next to the city of Quito. It pitted a Patriot army under General Antonio José de Sucre against a Royalist army commanded by Field Marshal Melchor Aymerich. The defeat of the Royalist forces loyal to Spain brought about the liberation of Quito.

pronounced. Suddenly, on a sharp bend in the road, the full vista of that great, flat river basin lay before them[6].

"There is a small village just a few kilometres ahead down on the plain. There Conchita and I will leave you and I will return here and stay at the farmhouse of one of my flock until the villagers tell me of your return. I know these people well and they will also be happy to see a 'Black Robe' again, Brother Xavier, as there was once a Jesuit Mission here before the Expulsion. They are the Kichwa People who speak a form of the widely-spoken Incan language of Quechua. We will be able to negotiate a canoe to take you and the good colonel downstream to your destination – of which I know nothing, of course," he said the last words with a wink of his eye. There was little that Brother Dom did not know, especially about the local

---

[6] This is at the current Mirador (lookout) Mira Mera on the eastern slopes of the Andes.

people and the country to the south where they were going.

They reached the small settlement just before nightfall and were greeted by a large man who was obviously from the local tribe. Whilst he wore the white habit of the Dominicans, albeit rather grubby in many places, he also wore a small headdress of feathers and had facial tattoos across his forehead and cheeks which were painted in yellow and blue stripes. He greeted Brother Dom with a great hug which lifted the smaller man off the ground. Still somewhat shaken, Brother Dom turned to his too friends and exclaimed:

"This is our Lay Brother Guillermo and this is his small mission. He tends to his peoples' care and tries to teach them some Spanish. He also tends to their spiritual needs but he has been befriended by a local old brujo[7] and I am told that he has been initiated into their snake clan, so who knows what that may be?"

Brother Guillermo gave a toothless grin and eagerly hugged both Xavier and Colonel Ernesto in term. "Welcome, Señores to Uchuy llaqta Santiago[8]". I see that you bring a 'Black Robe' with you?" he said looking at Xavier with an uncertain smile.

Xavier took a step forward and put his hand on the big man's shoulder: "Anchatam kusikusani riqsisuspayki[9]" He said in Quechua."

---

[7] Brujo: the Spanish term for a sorcerer, wizard, or witch doctor; a man who practises magic.

[8] Quechua: Small village of Santiago or Saint James.

[9] Quechua: "Pleased to meet you."

"Ah, he speaks the Runasimi[10]? That is good." clasping Xavier's shoulder with his hand also. "Come up to the house and we will have some chicha[11]".

Xavier looked around and saw that the settlement consisted of several small, wooden and thatched huts which stood mostly on the river bank. They had floors made of the same dark red clay that formed the bank. Several people stood nearby; some women standing close to one of the further huts, one holding a small child and some men who stood in a small group warily watching the strangers who had just arrived from the mountains.

Brother Guillermo's house was a little more substantial, being raised up on wooden stumps, but it still consisted of only one room with a small landing at the top of the

----

[10] "The people's tongue" is how the Quechua-speaking people refer to their language.
[11] Fermented corn beer.

steps. Inside, there was only the minimal number of furnishings with a tired old chest of drawers, a small table and two chairs, a large wooden crucifix on the opposite wall and a large, woven hammock stretching across one corner.

Xavier and Colonel Ernesto pulled up the chairs and sat down. Brother Dom sat on the edge of the table and wasted little time in explaining why they had come down from the mountains. They were to rescue some captured patriots from the Peruvians and to bring them back home. They would need a good canoe and strong, experienced paddlers to take then down the Río Pastaza to somewhere near a small village belonging to the Achuar people and then return. The distance would be no more than about one hundred kilometres and would probably take about two or three days downstream and possibly twice that time coming back.

They would need supplies for about six or seven days.

Brother Guillermo paced up and down his small hut in silence for a while and then sat in his hammock. He looked at Brother Dom with some concern and then said. "The Achuar are not civilized! There has been some peace on the river for a while, but they resent any strangers coming into their lands. The Black Robes were there for a while but left or were killed. Who knows? It will not be an easy journey, my friends."

"But can you help us, Brother Guillermo?" Colonel Ernesto asked.

There was more pacing and silence and then Brother Guillermo turned and said with a wicked smile across his face: "Yes! I will go with you. I have four stout men from this village who will come as well. We are not afraid of the Achuar! But for now, we will have chicha and some food."

With that he ran down the steps calling out in Quechua for one of the women, who obviously carried out his domestic duties, to bring food and chicha.

The sun sets rapidly in the jungle here abouts and soon Brother Guillermo returned with a woman who carried bowls of various foods, mostly yams and plantains[12] baked in the coals, some form of meat, and a large earthenware jug of chicha with some cups of the same material. He also warned us never to drink the water from the jungle but to only drink chicha or very strong black coffee. Some vines, he said could also be slashed and the juice drunk, but not the ones which had a milky sap as they were poisonous. Even the morning dew or rain falling through some trees, such as the *Sachacurarine*

---

[12] A type of green banana used in cooking.

palm, is poisonous and will burn the skin on contact but, he added with a grin, the local people can use its sap to cure snake bite.

An old paraffin lamp was lit and hung from a hook hanging from the roof. Two more hammocks were strung across the opposite corners and Brother Guillermo placed an old straw mattress for himself along the narrow landing in front of the door. He also produced several fine-mesh nets which he strung up over the hammocks to give some protection from mosquitoes and other night insects. The insects, even at this hour, were a bother to Xavier who had spent most of his life in the cool, dry air of the Altiplano. Perhaps these nets may offer some comfort, but then perhaps not. Brother Guillermo also produced a small earthenware jar which contained an evil-looking red oil.

"Urucul" said Brother Guillermo, smearing some of it onto the backs of his hands and face and then offering it to Xavier. "It is made from the *Achiote* plant, this will keep the insects away, but do not let it get into your eyes."

Xavier took a little of the oil and smeared it across his cheeks and on the backs of his hand.

"We must sleep now," said Brother Guillermo. "There is very little for us to do tonight and the jungle is a dangerous place at this time."

He waited until his three guests had removed their top clothing and climbed under the nets into their hammocks. Xavier noticed that underneath his cassock, Brother Dom wore pantaloons, a long-sleeved shirt and long socks, which he had tucked into the bottoms of his pantaloons so that only his head and hands were exposed. These also had been smeared with the red oil.

Brother Guillermo extinguished the lantern and moved out onto the landing. In parting he said: "Remember to check your boots in the morning. There are spiders and small snakes which like to use them for shelter. Good night."

Capítulo Once:
El Río de la Vida y la Muerte
(Chapter Eleven: The River of Life and
Death)

Xavier woke with a start. The grey light of
the early morning was slowly creeping into
the hut when he felt a light touch to his face.
He turned his head suddenly to see two
bright eyes looking at him through the insect
net. They were set in a small, black face and
a long, black finger was tracing itself along
the edge of his hammock. As he suddenly sat
up, the apparition jumped back with an
excited cry and dashed from the room.
Xavier just had a fleeting impression of a
long-legged black creature with long arms
waving over its head which ran screeching
through the open door.

Untangling himself from the netting which
had fallen down during his struggle, he ran
to the door only to be greeted by Brother

Guillermo who was coming up the steps. He laughed at Xavier's expression of shock: "Ah! I see that you have met our Lorenca?" he said as he handed Xavier a steaming cup of strong coffee.

"What was that?" Xavier said, trying to calm his nerves and sitting down on the edge of the landing. Brother Guillermo also sat down next to him and put his arm around his shoulders.

"She was Lorenca. A spider monkey who often comes into our camp. She belongs to a small group of monkeys which seemed to have adopted us here in our little village. They are still wild monkeys, you understand, but the children feed them and so they often visit."

Xavier gave a small laugh, now embarrassed at his first meeting with Lorenca who seemed to have just been curious about the newcomer in Brother Guillermo's hut.

"Look!" said Brother Guillermo, pointing to some trees near the edge of the village. "There she is with her friends."

Xavier followed Brother Guillermo's pointing finger and saw movement in the trees. There were indeed several monkeys now playing in the branches; two lithe black spider monkeys and a smaller, brown monkey which he recognised as a Capuchin. As he sipped his coffee, Xavier watched as several children from the village came over to the tree and offered the monkeys some nuts which they had gathered. The Capuchin led the way down from the tree followed by the two Spider Monkeys.

He could see now, why they were so called. Their fur was black and they had very long limbs which seemed to be disproportionate to their bodies. They moved about upright on their hind legs, with their arms held up high for balance standing about a metre tall. Xavier smiled as he was reminded of some aerial tight-rope walker carefully treading along a narrow wire using his arms in just such a manner. The smaller of the two black monkeys, whom Xavier felt was his morning wakener, Lorenca, found an old wooden tub where she seated herself to survey what was going on in the village. She was very much the village 'grand dame' who missed nothing. The other Spider Monkey took food from the children and rolled over in several small cartwheel tumbles to gain more attention.

Now assured of the relatively safety of the morning, Xavier finished his coffee before going inside to dress; remembering to check the insides of his boots for any unpleasant occupant.

Colonel Ernesto and Brother Dom came in and passed some remark about the leisure of the Jesuits referring to the lateness of the morning which really, from Xavier's point of view, had yet to dawn.

Now dressed, he followed his two friends out of the hut and down to the river. Here he was surprised to find that all preparations for their expedition had already been completed. There was a long dugout canoe which seemed to be about ten metres long sitting on the long slope which went down to the water from the high bank above. Near it were four Kichwas; strong looking men, tall with broad shoulders. They had painted their bodies and their faces and wore only simple loin cloths or the remains of European pants. Apart from their friendly grins, they looked every inch the warriors whom Xavier had heard stories about in his childhood.

He was handed a small bowl of fruit by one of the women who had come down to see the party leave on their journey down the Río Pastaza and turned as he heard some low cries of appreciation behind him. Brother Guillermo was walking down towards them but he was now someone else. He wore only a loincloth and his body was extensively painted. His face and headdress remained as they were the day before, but without his Dominican cassock; the rest of his huge muscular body was now completely painted. His arms and legs were painted in a deep blue, but his chest was painted in a bright yellow and down this background was painted a long, twisting snake in black and red. He was no longer Brother Guillermo, a Lay Brother of the Dominican order but an initiated sorcerer of the Snake Clan, demanding fear and respect.

He grinned when he came up to Xavier and said in a conspiratorial way: "Down the river, we will have no trouble, for all those on the Río Pastaza fear the power of the Snake Clan."

It was time to go. Brother Dom came down and embraced Xavier, Colonel Ernesto and Brother Guillermo and then stood back to say: "I will also go now. Back to my beloved mountains. Conchita and I are used to the clean air above, not this thick, hot air which comes from the damp of the forest. We will go back to a friendly farmhouse I know not far past the mirador. Jorge there has a good kitchen, two strong mules and a large cart to take what you bring back. The Kichwa will notify me when you return, so until then, ve con Dios!"

Brother Dom then turned away and went up to the hut to make preparations for his own departure.

Several of the men from the village came down to the water's edge to help their four companions launch the big canoe. The four warriors climbed in and assisted Xavier and Colonel Ernesto to take their seats at the centre of the craft. Brother Guillermo stood near the canoe and made some dramatic movements with a large gourd from which he sprinkled water on both the canoe and its occupants. Higher up on the bank, the women of the village, both old and young, formed a long line and began to chant a rhythmic song whilst the men came down to the water's edge and linked their arms and began to dance and stamp their feet to the music whilst uttering various guttural sounds.

The canoe with its occupants, baskets and jugs of food and water was now pushed out into the current of the Río Pastaza as their expedition began[13].

The Río Pastaza at this point, not far from where it emerges from the steep valleys of the mountains, still flowed at a fast rate and had not yet freed itself from the many rounded boulders which formed small rapids here and there. The four paddlers whooped and yelled at each other to avoid these dangerous rocks. There were two paddlers at the rear to help steer the canoe and two in the very bow to paddle frantically backwards or sideways to prevent collisions with any of the rocks or floating debris. Their huge muscles bunched up and then stretched out as they paddled the speeding canoe around the obstacles. Occasionally, the nose of the canoe would dig into a swirling wave drenching Xavier and Colonel Ernesto with

---

13 Travel with the author, down the Rio Madre de Dios, another headwater of the Amazon in southern Peru. See: https://www.youtube.com/watch?v=VhJ7Ve1FbL0

water. Brother Guillermo sat near the rear of the canoe so that he could see everything. He sang out loudly with a long cry of exhilaration every time water broke over the canoe. Xavier and Colonel Ernesto clung to both sides of the canoe with some trepidation and without the confidence of the others.

After several hours, the direction of the river suddenly changed from the southeast to the east. Here it began to widen and form several braided streams across its broad course. Keeping in the main channel, the warriors now had to exert some strength in keeping the canoe up to its frantic speed but there were fewer obstacles.

Eventually, the river seemed to widen slightly, stretching to one main channel. It was relatively easy going for the four paddlers and the three passengers, although Brother Guillermo seemed to be more at home in the stretch of wild water. He had been quietly chanting to himself near the canoe's stern. Xavier was not sure as to whether or not these were prayers to a protective saint or incantations to some river spirit. No matter what he thought; they were probably both for the same purpose in the Dominican's mind.

Eventually the river turned suddenly once more to resume its south-easterly course. Xavier had been completely enthralled with the scenery and the river; he had never been into any rainforest before, having spent all of his life in the mountains or on the narrow western plains at the foot of the Andes. Now this was a new world to him. The river had slowed down as they entered a section of sand bars in the centre of the river so they paddled closer to the shore. Xavier had time to look more closely at the forest and some of its creatures. He had imagined that the rainforest consisted of nothing but tall trees, but here on the river, the water gave way to a wide swath of tall reeds with vine-covered trees of only moderate height.

Occasionally the reeds would give way and the river would come up to a steep bank of light-coloured earth. On one bend he saw a small, roughly made hut on stilts which came out from the river bank. It was deserted but there were signs that its occupants were nearby as smoke curled slowly up from a stone fireplace on the bank.

"The people are wary of anyone on the river." Brother Guillermo said quietly as though he did not wish them to hear.

There was an abundance of bird life in the trees, and across a wide bar, some tall birds were wading in the shallows. Brother Guillermo took great delight in pointing some of the more obvious birds out: there was the quick kingfisher, with its bright blue wings, darting here and there into the water;

there was the stately cocoi heron wading in a pool looking for crustaceans; and high in a branch of a dead tree hanging over the water was a black caracara – the Amazonian falcon – with its curved beak and shiny black plumage.

Brother Guillermo held up his hand for silence. The warriors stopped paddling so that the canoe now drifted silently past the dense green foliage. "Listen!" said Brother Guillermo, holding his finger to his lips.

Xavier listened and slowly he began to hear a faint raucous squabbling which became louder as they approached a section of the forest denser than before. The leaves and lower branches of one tree were being agitated by several large, birds which were the strangest creatures that Xavier had ever seen.

"This the hoatzin[14]," said Brother Guillermo, "the noisiest bird in the forest. Look at him! Is he not a strange bird?"

Indeed, Xavier did think that this bird, now seen as one of a family of three who fought for a position on a lower branch, was the strangest that he had ever seen.

It was about the size of a large chicken, with large wings which were a rusty brown underneath and a bulky body to match and a long white neck. The top of the wings and body were a grey colour streaked with white and the birds regularly opened and closed their wings in excitement.

It was the head of the bird which was its strangest attribute; being bare and blue-white with a short beak and large red eyes. On top of its head was a large crest of long

---

[14] The hoatzin (*Opisthocomus hoazin*) - pronounced *wat-sin* – has many characteristics of the first birds of from 150 to 125 million years ago.

orange feathers which were constantly being raised up like some spikey fan. Their raucous series of clucking sounds was loud and constant as they fought over their position on the branch. Suddenly one flew off and Xavier was astonished that such a large bird could actually fly, but gliding was probably a more appropriate description.

"You know," said Brother Guillermo," that the younger birds have claws on their wings so that they can climb back up the tree if they should fall from their nest. Most strange."

Having passed this noisy family of ancient birds, the canoe now encountered a huge lagoon jutting into the forest which now showed its tall species. The entire far side of this lagoon was ringed with immensely tall açai palms and behind them stood even taller, hardwood trees topped with a dense canopy of foliage, vines and epiphytes[15].

"Look there!" called Colonel Ernesto who was now pointing towards a ripple in the water in the still lagoon. Soon another appeared and then a round grey head appeared above the surface. The animal then dived below revealing a sleek, grey and shiny body.

"Patrón[16], that is what the Achuar people call *wankanim* but which we call in Spanish the *lobo de río* or 'the river wolf'. You may know it as the giant otter. Look there! It has dived and caught a fish!"

Sure enough, the large grey, furry head had returned to the surface with a huge fish in its

---

[15] An epiphyte is a plant that grows on the surface of another plant, often high in the canopy and derives its moisture and nutrients from the air, rain, or from debris accumulating around it.

[16] Generally used here for patron or 'boss'.

mouth. It swam over to the side of the lagoon not far from where the canoe now drifted and the otter beat the fish on a rock which had been exposed there. It then set about eating it.

"You see!" said Brother Guillermo, "the otter will live because the fish has died. It is all the same along this river of life and death. And in the forest too. Even the trees die that others may live."

It was a simple statement of natural philosophy which could be applied to anywhere, but here in the steamy heat of the rainforest it was shown with brutal reality.

"Is it the same with the people who live here?" asked Colonel Ernesto.

"Si, Patrón." Brother Guillermo replied. "We all must live and of course we will die. There are many things in the forest which see us as food, and of course we often must fight for land so that our people can live. This why your people have often come into our forests and have never returned."

The last comment was followed by a wicked grin which made Colonel uneasy. Brother Guillermo may be a Lay Dominican but he was also a Kichwa brujo who would naturally resent any massive encroachment into his people's territory.

"Your people seem friendly enough!" said Colonel Ernesto in response and Brother Guillermo replied:

"That is true Patrón, they have heard a little of God's kindness and it makes sense to us in a hostile world. We see some of the advantages of contact with your people but not if you wish to take over our land. It is the same with the other peoples on this river, but they have had little contact with the outside world."

"And what of these people further down the river? Are they dangerous?" Colonel Ernesto asked.

Si, Patrón." Brother Guillermo replied, "very dangerous. Many of your people have gone further down the Río Pastaza and have never come back. Even the Kichwa do not venture far from their own lands. We will soon be in the lands of the Shuar peoples and then into that of the Achuar. The Spaniards and now your people often refer to both these peoples as Jívaro; but that word has come to mean 'savage' and they consider it an insult. The Shuar are head-takers. They sometimes go on raids, especially into Achuar lands, and take as many heads of their enemies as they can. They then retreat into their own land and change the heads into grapefruit-sized 'tsantsa' or 'shrunken heads' as you would say. They do this by removing the skull, sewing up the lips and packing the skin with sand before boiling and drying. These fresh tsantsa are then worn around the warriors' necks as the Shuar believed that humans have three souls, one of which – called the 'muisak' – is charged with avenging the victim's death. The only way to pacify the enraged soul and protect themselves, they believe is to shrink the deceased's head, as this contained the victim's soul."

Colonel Ernesto looked at Xavier with a grimace: "I think that we have a better way of placating the soul. Don't you?"

"That is true Patrón, but this is the way of the jungle and it is difficult to argue with such traditions, especially when your congregation is looking for heads." Brother Guillermo gave a little laugh and continued: "The Shuar do not generally believe in natural death. Any unexplained death is attributed to what they call 'tsentsak' – the spearing with spiritual darts which cannot seen. This can be the act of a 'Uwishin' – their word for a brujo - who possess and controls tsentsak and they believe that the most powerful shamans are Quichua-speakers like myself, so we will have no trouble with them".

"Tell me more about the Achuar?" Xavier asked. Brother Guillermo looked at Xavier with a wicked grin and said:

"The Achuar people are also one of the fiercest in the forest and they too will shrink the heads of their enemies. Like the Shuar, they generally wish to be left alone and live their life in the forest of which they are a part. To us, they are called the 'dream people' because their culture uses many dreams and visions so that they can talk to the spirits of the jungle – the animals, the trees and all that is around them. They are all one. If they and the Shuar are considered savages, it is because outsiders come and destroy them and the sprits of their lands."

"And what do you believe, Brother Guillermo?" Xavier asked.
The painted brujo looked at Xavier and grinned: "I am a good Christian, my brother. However, there are things in this forest which are difficult to understand by one such as you. The very forest has a spirit or a soul if you will. Sometimes it is unseen - just the feeling which you have when you go into the dark forest and you feel the hair rise on the back of your neck. Sometimes it is in the form of a powerful brujo who can move quickly and unseen through the jungle. The people who live here call him Chullachaqui – the Jungle Spirit, and he is usually death to them".

"Yes, I have heard of him," said Xavier, "but perhaps the good colonel has not. Please continue Brother Guillermo."

"Patrón," Brother Guillermo continued, turning to look at Colonel Ernesto, "you need to know what this word 'Chullachaqui' means, for it is not just a spirit living in the jungle, for there are many of these; it is the very spirit and life of the jungle itself. It can be a very good spirit for those who know and practice its ways, but for a puningare[17], or a stranger like yourselves, it can be a very bad spirit which is with you all the time you are in his land.

Suddenly one of the paddlers called out and pointed excitedly into the centre of the river. There, following his outstretched arm, Xavier saw another animal swimming. From what he could see out of the water, the

---

17. ["Poonin-GAH-reey"] local term for a stranger, a gringo!

animal had red-brown fur and seemed to be over a metre in length.

"Capybara!" cried Brother Guillermo who reached down and pulled up his spear from the bottom of the canoe as the paddlers turned it towards the swimming animal.
It was a good swimmer but soon the canoe came up to the animal and Brother Guillermo speared it and threw it into the bottom of the boat. It thrashed there for a few seconds and then went still. Xavier saw that it was longer than he thought; more like one and a half metres long. He had never seen a capybara before but knew from his natural history classes that it was a member of the rodent family and often considered good eating by the peoples of the Amazon region.

It was getting later in the afternoon and the canoe was paddled over to a large playa[18] on

____

[18] Spanish: 'beach'. In this case a large point bar of sand on a river.

the inside bend of the river. The canoe was paddled right up onto the shore until there was a crunch of sand beneath it. The two paddlers in the bow of the canoe jumped out and pulled it further up onto the sand to allow the others to get out.

The four warriors and Brother Guillermo now pulled out the supplies which they would need for the night and began to set up camp. Colonel Ernesto walked over the sand and stood back from the tight foliage of the forest and resettled his pistol in its holster. The good soldier, he was very unsure of the safety of such a camp. Xavier, too was apprehensive but stood and watched his companions. Eventually, two of the warriors picked up their spears and went across the broad playa and into the jungle to fetch firewood.

Brother Guillermo came up to Xavier and nodded in the direction that the two warriors had disappeared into the dense green curtain. "It will be dark soon and the warriors will not stay for long in the jungle. There are too many harmful things there and they are also afraid of Chullachaqui."

Soon the warriors returned with armfuls of dry wood which they had broken off from dead trees, not wishing to pick up wood from the floor of the forest. Soon they had a roaring fire going and Brother Guillermo had returned to the canoe to cut up the poor capybara. He did so and went over to the fire to impale some of the great slabs of meat onto sticks which he repositioned over the fire. What happened next was a revelation to both Xavier and Colonel Ernesto.

Brother Guillermo returned to the canoe and then took up the remains of the capybara and another spear which had several prongs at its end- a fishing spear. He looked up at Xavier and grinned. "Now you will see our dreaded man-eating fish, the piraña[19]"

He walked down to the water's edge and threw the carcass well out into the river. Xavier had heard fanciful stories of these 'devil fish' who attacked their victim in great numbers and could strip the flesh of a large animal in seconds.

Now as night was falling fallen, to Xavier's surprize, Brother Guillermo took a well-lit torch from the fire and walked right out into the river almost up to his waist. He carried the remains of the capybara carcass in one hand and his fishing spear in the other. Standing very still, he threw the carcass downstream and then raised his spear well above his head ready to strike. He struck suddenly and quickly retreated back to the shore, a small writhing silver fish on the end of his spear.

---

[19] Pronounced 'piranya'

"Tonight, we eat capybara, but tomorrow you will see a man eating fish – six of us- ha! ha!" He laughed at his own play on words.

He explained that, unlike the ill-informed opinion of those who never ventured into the Amazon Basin, piraña will not attack humans unless they are agitated or if the river is drying up and food is scarce. Standing still and with a diversion downstream, such as the bleeding capybara carcass, one is able to spear the fish at night. Although, he cautioned, one does not venture into the water if one is bleeding. It was his intention to catch several this way and then smoke them over the fire, for they made very good eating[20].

---

[20] The author's son once caught piraña using a line in the Río Madre de Dios in Peruvian Amazonia and then used them to make ceviche – the Peruvian national dish. See here for a recipe (other white fish can be used):
https://www.feastingathome.com/easy-ceviche-recipe/

Our four warriors had collected enough firewood for a substantial fire and Xavier and his friends had an excellent dinner of capybara meat, yams and some nuts which Brother Guillermo had collected from the forest. He then hung the filleted fish over a green branch above the fire and threw some leaves of particular herbs, which he had also collected, onto the fire to 'add some flavour' he said.

In the firelight, his body size and painting made a fearsome appearance, and Xavier could understand why the local people would be afraid of the Clan of the Snake. It would be safe to sleep here on the sand, he had added, as the firelight would keep away any passing caiman[21] and the smoke, now pungent with the smell of his herbal additives would also keep away the night insects. Xavier and Colonel Ernesto found a

---

[21] Caiman are Amazonian relatives of the alligator and can grow up to four metres in length.

place near the fire and, being trained to live in the field as soldiers, dug small hollows for their shoulders and hip. It was a warm night so that they only needed their cloaks for covering. Brother Guillermo and three of the warriors also found good sleeping positions near the fire, the fourth warrior would take his turn at watch and to add fuel to the fire as it died down. Sleep was welcome as it had been a long and exhausting day.

For the next few days, the party made excellent time down the Río Pastaza. In the morning, the sun rose as filtered light streamed through the forest; often associated with a dense fog which soon cleared. On the morning of their third day, they were treated to the curious sight of brilliantly coloured parrots and macaws licking the clay on the steep river bank opposite. Brother Guillermo explained that the nuts that these birds usually preferred were normally poisonous and that the birds had found that the minerals in these clays would neutralize these toxins.

They had made good time with the fast-flowing current such that Brother Guillermo thought that now they must be in Achuar territory. They had seen no sign of human life on the river bank and their guide had explained that he had heard that these people shunned the major rivers as a protection against raids from other tribes and from mosquitoes; preferring instead to build on small streams or lakes.

Xavier had just woken after a fitful night on the edge of a large playa and was now stowing some of their supplies into the canoe when a large, black arrow suddenly embedded itself into the side of the canoe with a loud 'thunk!' Instinctively he dropped to the ground as did his companions when they heard his cry of warning and saw the arrow sticking out of the canoe's side.

Capítulo Doce:
Los Guerreros de las Palmas
(Chapter Twelve: The Warriors of the Palms)

The sudden appearance of the long, black arrow into the side of the canoe put everyone into a state of fear. Colonel Ernesto pulled his pistol out of its holster where it had been placed on his coat, and the four warriors fell to the ground and crawled across the sand to seek the protection of the canoe. Brother Guillermo, on the other hand stood erect with his arms outstretched on either side of his body so that whoever fired the arrow would see his body markings as brujo in the early morning light. Quietly he said to Xavier and Colonel Ernesto:

"If they wanted to kill us, we would all be full of arrows by now. Stand up and show them that you are not afraid."

This was difficult for Xavier to do but he stood up and so did Colonel Ernesto. The warriors maintained their positions in the sand behind the canoe. Brother Guillermo called out loudly in his own tongue which was a form of Quechua so that Brother Xavier understood what he said. He was saying that he was a brujo of the Snake Clan as they could see unless they were stupid, or blind men and therefore our party was under the protection of the Chullachaqui. Death to those who abuse this favour.

There was silence from the forest. Slowly, our paddlers stood up, comforted now by Brother Guillermo's words and the lack of arrows coming from the trees. Suddenly, a tall warrior stepped slowly out from the foliage at the edge of the forest at the far side of the playa well downstream. He was not as broad as Brother Guillermo, but was still impressive with bold patterns tattooed across his broad face and chin, he wore headdress of red, black and yellow woven toucan feathers. "What you want here, Brother Snake?" he said in broken Quechua. "Go from our land!"

Xavier stepped forward and spoke up in Quechua: "We are sorry to be on your land. We seek your help in taking away some puningare who have also come into your land and are held captive by another of my tribe."

There was silence and the Achuar warrior turned and walked back into the forest. Brother Guillermo walked slowly up behind Xavier and lightly put his hand onto his shoulder.

"They are thinking about what you have said. Our friend seems to have learnt some of my language through some contact with my people – probably captives which they have taken long ago. We must wait, for they often need some dreaming guidance before making a decision." With that, he squatted down onto the sand and bade Xavier to do the same. Behind them, Colonel Ernesto and the Kichwa warriors did likewise.

After what seemed to be an incredibly long time, the tall warrior appeared and raised his right hand above his head. He again called out in broken Quechua:

"We will help. But only the yurak runakuna.[22] Brujo and braves stay!"

Colonel Ernesto looked inquisitively at Brother Guillermo who simply nodded his head. "It will be well, Patrón. They would not harm a friend of the Snake Clan and once help is offered, it is their custom, like most of us here in the forest, to give protection and hospitality as well. Go with them, we will set up camp here and wait five days."

---

[22] Kichwa: 'white people'.

Colonel Ernesto again nodded his head, put his pistol back into its holster and went to the canoe to fetch his things. Xavier followed and did likewise. Xavier and Colonel Ernesto walked across the broad playa and Xavier turned and waved farewell to Brother Guillermo.

The tall Achuar warrior looked at Xavier then down at his black cassock then at Colonel Ernesto. He suddenly turned and went into the forest. Xavier and Colonel Ernesto followed and found a group of five other warriors standing silently amongst the trees. Their leader said a few words to them in their own language and they turned and walked off into the jungled at a fast stride. Xavier and Colonel Ernesto followed, finding the pace rather faster than what they were accustomed to.

There was a track of sorts through the jungle which followed the river at some distance.

The party continued for some time until suddenly the leader stopped. He raised his hand that all should stop and be silent. He motioned for Xavier and Colonel Ernesto to come forward and then he pointed down in front of him.

Moving across the barely-defined track appeared to be a wide, brown, jostling river. It was about a metre wide and extended into the jungle on both sides of the track.

Colonel Ernesto looked past the warrior and exclaimed: "Marabunta!"

Xavier had head of these 'soldier ants' which would often swarm through the jungle as a living river of bodies, moving from one nest to another. This appeared to be only a small swarm as he had heard that often the body of ants could be several metres wide.

"They are said to be able to cover a human body and strip it of its flesh in minutes, but that is only a good tale to scare children. Its sting, however is very painful so take care where you walk," said Colonel Ernesto.

The warriors quickly jumped over the swarm and continued on their way, through stands of tall palms, past trees with trunks covered in vicious-looking spikes and at all times, many large, snake-like vines hanging down from the tall trees above. As they moved away from the river, many of the trees became extremely tall, held into the thin soil by large buttress roots jutting out like the supports of some gothic cathedral.

On one occasion, they emerged into a clearing where a large tree had fallen over. Many smaller trees and bushes now grew in the space where the giant had cleared the forest in its fall. There were many colonies of fungi of different sizes, shapes and colour now breaking the giant's body down to bare fibre. The dead help to create new life thought Xavier.

The sunlight in the clearing now came down in vertical streams through the steamy air of the forest suggesting to Colonel Ernesto that it was about midday. They had been travelling now for several hours.

Suddenly they broke out from the trees into a wide clearing with grass and a tall line of fences made from bound wooden stakes of palm trees beyond. This was the village of the local Achuar people.

The leader stopped and called out in his own language to those in the village and was answered by a returning cry in the same tongue. A gate, indiscernible from the rest of the fence opened to allow the party to enter.

The leader led his warriors into the village, which he called Shimigae, now walking proudly to show his people his new 'guests'.

Xavier looked with considerable interest at houses of the village. Each house was shaped as a large oval, most without outer walls to allow ventilation. They had a high roof with straight sides which were made out of palm tree[23] fronds with palm trunks used for house beams. There were large yards and gardens surrounding many of the homes. The size of a house plays a pivotal part in the ego of an Achuar man. They came up to a bigger house in the centre of a large space which was what the tall warrior now said as that of a juunt, or great man. It had walls of palm fronds woven together.

He motioned them to stop and wait. Soon, an old man emerged from an opening made by pushing aside some of the palm fronds. He

---

[23] The name Achuar means 'the people of the aguaje palm'

was probably once a tall warrior like the others, but now he was bent and his skin very wrinkled. He had the usual facial tattoos and headdress of the others but also wore many rows of highly covered beads around his neck and down his chest.

The tall warrior began a long speech which Xavier felt must be some form of introduction along with the brave acts of the warriors in coming upon these strangers and offering them hospitality.

The old man listened whilst carefully examining the two strangers from head to foot. He was especially interested in Xavier and reached out and touched his cassock. The tall warrior turned to Xavier and said in his broken Quechua"

"Our older brother asks if you are a brujo of the Black Robes whom he saw as a young man?"

Xavier was rather taken back by this statement so he simply turned to the old man and bowed his head. The old man smiled and then swept his arm out towards a woven palm mat which had been placed in front of the hut; a sign that the two strangers should be seated.

By now, a large crowd had gathered and were standing at some respectful distance in a semi-circle around the tall warrior, his elder and the two seated strangers. A woman brought a large bowl containing a milky substance and was directed by the elder to offer it first to Xavier.

"Nijiamanch[24]" said the tall warrior who motioned with his hands that Xavier should drink. It was bitter to the taste but Xavier felt that it would be an insult if he refused. He took a long sip of the bitter liquid without

[24] This is produced by the women of the village, who chew manioc roots, which they then spit into a bowl – the saliva aids fermentation – much like kava of the Pacific islands.

any sign of emotion and passed it over to Colonel Ernesto with a nod that he should do the same.

Having satisfied the villager's offering of hospitality and curiosity, the tall warrior motioned for the two guests to stand and having made a short bow towards the elder, headed off to the main gate. Their trek through the jungle now resumed.

It was not long until the warrior stopped within sight of the river. It was a secluded inlet covered completely with vines and other foliage. There were several small canoes pulled well from the bank and one had a set of paddles. He pushed aside some branches and pointed downstream, turning to look at Xavier. Colonel Ernesto walked cautiously forward and pulled a small pocket telescope out of his jacket and looked in the direction in which the warrior had pointed.

"A stockade!" he exclaimed and turned to Xavier and handed him the telescope. There, about two hundred metres downstream on the opposite bank of the Río Pastaza, was indeed a rough stockade of lashed vertical poles. From a taller pole within the stockade flew the red and white vertically-striped flag of Peru. He turned to find that the warrior had gone, leaving the two men on the river bank alone.

Capítulo Trece:
Resurrección
(Chapter Thirteen: Resurrection)

Together, they pushed the small canoe through the foliage and down a natural slope in the river bank. Dragging the canoe across a small sand bar, they pushed into the still water and Xavier climbed in and moved to the bow. Colonel Ernesto sat in the stern and pushed the craft out into the main flow of the river. By now, the Río Pastaza had quietened down into a broad, slow-flowing river, typical of many of the headwaters of the mighty Amazon.

After a while, Colonel Ernesto called out to Xavier: "We will be there soon and perhaps I should tell you the full story of our mission. You know that the Peruvians – your countrymen – have three of our soldiers somewhere in this region, most likely in this camp before us. Both our governments are embarrassed by this particular action and naturally want the affair – shall we say 'smoothed over'. It would be a disaster, both politically and militarily, if those seeking power in our country and especially the popular press, found out that we crossed the border and then left three men in the jungle and in the hands of the Peruvian military."

"A very delicate situation, Colonel." Xavier replied.

"Most delicate! So, you can see why there was not grand rescue and public outcry this time. Both governments wish to keep this retrieval a secret and this is why I sought you out. I knew from your military background – oh, yes, I did check on your earlier career with the 23rd Hussars – and as a Peruvian training in Ecuador as a priest is also very useful. Your knowledge of Quechua and your vocation has been most useful."

Approaching the stockade now, they heard the sound of a trumpet as the sentry on duty had obviously spotted the canoe carrying the two men down towards them. A small gate opened and a squad of soldiers, bayonets fixed, came out onto the river bank. Once they saw that it contained a high-ranking officer and a Jesuit brother, the rifles were lowered and several men quickly came down to help the canoe ashore. An officer busily pushed his way through the group, came to attention and gave a smart salute. Xavier thought that this ceremony seemed much too superfluous in the middle of a jungle.

The officer was a Capitán and for a moment he seemed to be lost for words; the expression on his face be one of disbelief. "Please come this way, Colonel." He said, pushing his way back through his men who had crowded the river bank to gawk at the two newcomers. They went up the river bank and into the stockade. Xavier was impressed by its size as it contained a wide Parade Ground not far from the river gate and a wide road going back through to another gate in the wooden wall in the distance. There were many rows of tents which would house at least a Company of men and Xavier noted with interest that only the small group who had come out to greet them wore infantry flashes on their blue field uniform; the rest of the soldiers who now came out of their tents wore the red and blue flashes of engineers.

They were led through the camp to a large tent sited not far from the central parade ground. One of its flaps was thrown open and a full colonel and a major emerged. The colonel came up to Colonel Ernesto and smiled:

"Ah, so you must be my counterpart in the Army of Ecuador come to assist me with this diplomatic mess?" he said with a smile. He was not a tall man, but was stocky and had the high cheek bones of a native of the Altiplano. His uniform was immaculate and he carried himself well. He put out his hand in friendship:

"Colonel Americo Serrano Tito of the Peruvian Army Exploration Department at your service." He said with a small bow and a sharp click of his heels.

"Military Intelligence" thought Xavier.

Colonel Ernesto also gave a short bow and replied: "Coronel Ernesto Robles Castro, of the Information Bureau of the Army of Ecuador."

"Military Intelligence" thought the Major who was standing back from his superior officer.

Colonel Ernesto stepped aside and indicated Xavier with his outstretch hand: "Allow me to present my good friend and confidant, Brother Xavier Aguirre del Río."

Xavier also gave a short bow.

"I know another of the name of 'Aguirre' - a Colonel Roberto Aguirre Montoya. A relative of yours perhaps?" Colonel Serrano asked.

"My father, Xavier confessed, confused that here, in the jungle was an acquaintance of his estranged father.

"Remarkable that here in the jungle I should meet the son of my old mentor at the Military Academy! How is the Colonel?"

Xavier replied with some sadness: "Alas, I have not seen my father in several years, but letters from my sister suggests that he is well."

"I am sorry to hear that, Brother Xavier." Colonel Serrano said solemnly but then looked up and smiled: "Well then Colonel Robles, we are in good, honest company! Colonel Aguirre was my instructor at the Military Academy and a man of exemplary character and honour. And now here is his son – a Jesuit. You have indeed brought a good man to assist you in our negotiations and I could use one such as he back at my headquarters. Come, now. Let us go into my canvas office – he laughed – and negotiate the release of these unfortunates of yours."

The colonel turned and went back under the flap into the large tent which had several camp beds and officers' campaign trunks as well as a long trestle table and collapsible chairs. Colonel Serrano offered Colonel Ernesto and Xavier two chairs opposite him across the table. The major went out and soon an orderly appeared with a jug of water and several glasses.

Colonel Serrano produced a sheath of papers from a leather shoulder bag and outlined the situation to Colonel Ernesto. Xavier kept his place and listened to the story which was briefly outlined:

"A party of your solders had ventured too far into Peruvian territory where this company of engineers were surveying a new road up from the south. The young officer of your army's reconnaissance party had come in from the headwaters of the Río Morona and had struck southeast where they encountered the track which our engineers were surveying north from Puerto Diaz along the Río Pastaza. Our small party of engineers were returning to this headquarters. There had been a brief exchange of gunfire. Unfortunately for your men, a sizeable party of infantry was coming up the track and quickly gave support. Our soldiers withdrew but three of them became disorientated in the forest and were captured by our troops.

When the Ecuadoran officer struggled back to his own Headquarters, he was able to send a telegraph signal on to Quito where your military headquarters was alerted. Naturally, they were not happy and neither were both our governments.

There has been considerable unrest in our country since the border war between our two countries had been concluded in 1860, and both governments did not want the more patriotic fanatics of our countries to demand another one. So, you see that if word got out about this small action, these hotheads could enflame both countries again into war."

Colonel Ernesto leaned across the table and said in almost a conspiratorial tone:

"I can see the problem clearly, Colonel Serrano. We have those sorts of people in our government as well. Such matters should be left to us simple soldiers who are usually left to clean up the mess once the 'sabre-rattlers' have finished their dirty work."

"You seemed to be a man after my own heart, Colonel Robles," replied Colonel Serrano. "So! Let us make a pact of silence and shake our hands upon it. As Brother Xavier is your friend, I have no doubt that your government will be happy with a soldier's apology and the return of these poor men to their families. I trust that the young officer concerned who strayed too far will be told to keep silent for the good of his country?"

"That he will, and probably a promotion to keep him happy," laughed Colonel Ernesto.

"Good! It is done, then!" said Colonel Serrano, standing up and opening up his campaign trunk to produce a good bottle of Peruvian wine.

"I am sure that Brother Xavier, who comes from an excellent military family, will join us in this solemn undertaking and share a glass of my good wine to seal the pact!"

Colonel Serrano poured a generous amount of his private stock of wine into the glasses and handed one each to Xavier and Colonel Ernesto: "Salud!" he said raising his glass.

Xavier and Colonel Ernesto had a few more glasses of Colonel Serrano's excellent wine and then were given over to the Major who took then across the parade Ground to another tent where the three Ecuadorean solders had been billeted. They had been afforded the same conditions as their Peruvian comrades but were first suspicious and then overjoyed as a full colonel of their army entered along with a Jesuit Brother.

Xavier raised his hand in peace, smiled and said that he had not come to give them the Last Rites, nor were they being shot for being captured. Instead, they would spend one more night here and then return to Ecuador with him the next day.

There is a sense of camaraderie between soldiers, even between enemies, and so that night a huge fire was built in the cleared space near the front gate and a celebration of farewell was given to the three soldiers by their former captors. Colonel Serrano produced some more of his excellent wine for his officers and his new guests and other bottles which, of course were not permitted in the soldiers' lines, suddenly appeared.

The next morning, still suffering from the previous night's hospitality, Xavier, Colonel Ernesto and the three Ecuadorean soldiers were escorted down to the river bank where their canoe had been prepared. It now contained several baskets of fruit, newly-baked bread, and of course some of Colonel Serrano's good wine. With a cheery farewell, the canoe was launched and their journey back up the Río Pastaza began.

It would take then all of that day to paddle upstream, but two more paddles had been found and with the three soldiers and some help from Xavier, they made good going up the slow-moving current. Xavier had the feeling, however that they were always being watched from the jungle which usually came right down to the edge of the water in most places. His senses were justified, for they had not paddled far when he saw the same tall, blue-painted warrior step out onto a small playa and raise his hand in acknowledgement that they were indeed truthful men and had found the lost members of their own tribe and were taking them out of his peoples' land.

It was coming onto darkness when they rounded a small bend in the river and Xavier saw the firelight coming from their familiar playa. They had returned.

Brother Guillermo strode down to the little, overcrowded canoe and threw his arms around Xavier in welcome. The three soldiers were extremely apprehensive when they saw Brother Guillermo's huge body and its snake markings, but soon introductions were made and they were embraced in their turn. Colonel Ernesto simply shook the big Dominican by the hand as he was weary and felt only like sleeping now that most of his troubles were over.

The rest of the return canoe trip up the Río Pastaza did not take as long as expected, now that they had several additional paddlers to push the canoe northwards. Several days later, they came up against the rapids, so Brother Guillermo suggested that they land and use a track which he knew well as he was now back in the land of his own people, the Kichwa. They walked for most of the day but were soon met by a large number of his people who had come out of the village to greet them. Word travels fast in the jungle.

There was much celebration in the Kichwa village that night and it was good to see Brother Guillermo now wearing the cassock of a Dominican Brother. Gone were the paint and beads and the Brotherhood of the Snake, hidden once more under the cassock of Christianity.

In the morning, Brother Dom arrived with a large mule cart being driven by another man who was introduced as Carlos, the farmer with whom Brother Dom had stayed during their adventure down the river. There were sad farewells as Colonel Ernesto, the three soldiers and Xavier joined Brother Dom and Carlos for the last leg of their return to Baños. Colonel Ernesto, the three soldiers and Xavier spent another enjoyable night at the Priory of the Dominicans with Brother Dom, his colleagues and the prior, who made them all comfortable.

The next morning, after a substantial breakfast, Carlos and Dom went back down the mountain to the farm where Dom was to retrieve his mule, Conchita; Colonel Ernesto and the three soldiers took the regular coach back to Ambato and its military headquarters; and Xavier settled down once more in the Dominican Priory to complete his period of Regency in Baños.

Time went quickly, as Xavier found that he spent most of his time with the old Dominican, Brother Dom in his travels around the farms and villages of the district. He had acquired an extra mule for Xavier to ride and both men were happiest when they were out in the countryside talking to the farmers and peoples of the villages. Xavier's knowledge of their customs was greatly improved and he found their way of life simple and rewarding. Of course, the 'old religion' of the Incas was never far from the thin veneer of Christianity which the Spaniards had imposed. The people were devout Christians, but it would be an unwise farmer who did not light a candle at Mass for the future of his crops and then return home and burn a llama foetus to ask Pachamama, the Earth goddess for the same bounty.

In Brother Dom, Xavier found a kindred spirit; he too preferred the independence of the open road and the countryside to the confines of a school or priory. The two men often talked about life amongst the people and the suffering that they sometimes had to endure at the hands of those in power in the cities.

Xavier's time of regency was suddenly shortened and he was called back to his Seminary in Cuenca. The Jesuit order had once more been targeted by elements of the government and their supporters who saw that their influence in protecting the common people had become an interference to their aspirations and exploitation. His further period of studies in theology leading to ordination was to be reduced in time but not in content. This meant that he spent much of his time at the seminary engaged in his studies and so time passed quickly.

In 1875, following the assassination of the conservative President Gabriel García Moreno on August 6th, things were becoming difficult for the order, so ordinations of the finishing students at the Seminary were planned for the following June. There was much excitement in the seminary as the date of ordination approached. Xavier was unexpectedly called upon to meet with the rector, Father Mateo and his mentor, Father Lorenzo.

In the rector's office, Xavier stood in front of the huge, carved wooden table and listened to Father Mateo who sat opposite and went through a number of papers on his desk. Father Lorenzo stood at some distance behind and to one side of his superior.

"Well, Brother Xavier." Father Mateo said, looking benignly over his glasses. "You have done well my son, and now we must send you out to do the work of the Lord. But where? You have shown many qualities which go beyond our usual candidates for priesthood. You have an excellent and enquiring mind but I doubt that being a teacher in one of our schools would suit your restless spirit."

Xavier was now becoming apprehensive. The future did not look good for the order and he had little control of his own future as a priest. Father Mateo went on:

"Your help in solving the case of the missing chalice and your expedition down the Río Pastaza on behalf of the military suggests that you would be more suited to do our work where your adventurous spirit would do the most good, both for the Church, the government and especially our people."

Xavier looked over at Father Lorenzo who returned his gaze with a discrete smile on his thin lips as Father Mateo continued:

"We have a mind to quietly attach you as a padre to the military headquarters in Quito.

Your good friend and mentor, Father Leon has suggested that such a placement would be most suitable to him, as he is now becoming too old for such a position and could do with some assistance. Moreover, we have had a request from Colonel Ernesto Robles that your guidance there would be much appreciated. It is also interesting to note that we also have had a remarkable letter of commendation from a Colonel Serrano of the Peruvian military who was impressed by your recent assistance down the Río Pastaza. It might mean that you may receive other such assignments which would help both the people and the Church in places far from your normal parish. Would such a posting be to your liking?"

Xavier now understood the meaning of this private meeting. He would be a padre to the Ecuadorian military where his connections and friendships would be of the best use. He would also be in a position to help the Jesuit order in the future to help to serve the common people at a time when its future looked uncertain.

"Thank you, Father Mateo. That would be most satisfactory," was all that Xavier could say. In himself, he was overjoyed with the freedom this gave him to serve those who needed him the most.

Father Mateo smiled and simply said: "Then so be it! Go now and prepare for your ordination."

Xavier and his three fellow brothers who were to be ordained, spent the night in Vigil in the Seminary's chapel. The next morning, they returned to their own cells where they washed and dressed in clean cassocks ready for the service. At the appropriate hour, they went to the chapel which was, by now, full of their guests and visiting clergy. Xavier had mixed feelings; he was alone and soon to be invested with considerable responsibility.

The four neophytes slowly processed down the aisle of the chapel in two lines behind the Crucifer, Thurifer and two brothers carrying the tall, golden candlesticks. It was Father Ambrose who led the procession and Xavier noted that both the Rector and the Father Provincial awaited them with the Bishop of Quito at the altar. Everyone in the chapel was standing but Xavier's mind was on keeping his composure.

They stood at some distance now from the altar. Each acolyte was then called forward and presented to the assembly. Xavier looked up and was overjoyed to see that his sister Gabriella and his younger brother Alejandro were standing in the first row of the congregation, their faces now beaming with their own happiness. Gabriella now had become a beautiful woman and stood proudly with her mantle over her head. His brother, Alejandro looked especially smart in the uniform of a Subteniente in the Peruvian Army. Tears came to Xavier's eyes when he saw that the tall man in the sombre black coat standing next to Gabriella was his father, Colonel Roberto Aguirre, the ghost of a smile upon his stern face.

Xavier now felt that he had been reconciled with his family and was truly reborn from the distressed fugitive with a life of uncertainty to a man now with a future and a mission at hand as Father Xavier, Jesuit priest.

Hernán Eduardo Moreno Ruiz is, like this story, fictional and is the nom de plume of Dr. Peter T. Scott, author of a number of books including the novels 'Letters from San Rafael' and its sequel 'Return to San Rafael'; in which the character of Father Xavier first appears.

Dr. Scott has many similarities to his fictional hero and was raised and educated in Sydney, Australia. Graduating as a Science Teacher in 1964, he began a successful career of over forty years in high schools and universities. Studying at various universities part time, he achieved a Bachelor of Science and Masters' Degrees in Science (Geology) and Educational Administration and finally a Doctorate in Education. He, too, volunteered for the Army Reserve in support of his friends who had been conscripted during the

Vietnam War and was commissioned into the reserve of the Australian Infantry.

After retiring from teaching in 2008, he visited many countries including South America several times. Here, he and his wife travelled extensively visiting, his daughter-in-law's family in the high Andes of Peru and many of the places mentioned in his books including those in Ecuador and Peruvian Amazonia.

Dr Scott at Baños de Agua Santa, 2011

He now lives in Brisbane, Australia with his wife and their sons and families and their grandchildren. He is the author of over twenty books on Earth Science, Environmental Science and several works of fiction.

Other Books by the Author
FICTION

Letters from San Rafael (as Hernan Moreno Ruiz). Set in South America in the 1880's, this is a collection of letters smuggled home by Don Hernan Moreno, an Intelligence officer of the Peruvian Army who has been captured by the Ecuadorans during a border dispute. Taken to the fortified hacienda in Baños, in the mountains of Ecudor, he and his sargeant, Garcia, are treated as honoured guests. Each of the ten stories tells of the life and times of people in the hacienda and beyond. The final chapter is the climax of the entire book.

Return to San Rafael is the sequel to LETTERS from SAN RAFAEL. It is now 1891 and it has been five years since Colonel Moreno and his faithful sergeant Garcia had escaped San Rafael. Now, Moreno receives a mysterious coded letter asking them to return to San Rafael to solve its secret and ensure the stability of both Ecuador and Peru.

The Ice Ship. Set mainly in the Antarctic in the 1840's, this is the story of the survival of the crew of the futuristic auxiliary steam whaler, the AUSTRALIS which has become trapped in the ice following its voyage south along the Antarctic Peninsula. Based upon actual observations and experience of the author during a 2011 voyage into the same region on a small ex-research vessel.

The Innocence of Tom Shipley is the first novel about young teacher Tom Shipley. It begins during his days at High School and his penchant as a Laboratory Prefect in making explosives and other prankish devices, follows him through similar acts at Teachers College and then out into his first appointment at age nineteen into the profession of teaching. At a brand-new school in Canberra, he finds that as the sole Science teacher, he is now the Acting Head of Department charged with establishing this subject at the school and equipping and managing several laboratories and new incoming staff.

Tom Shipley's War is a sequel to the INNOCENCE of TOM SHIPLEY and is about the young man's protest against those who protested about National Servicemen who were called up for the Vietnam War. He volunteers for the local Citizens' Military Forces unit (later the Army Reserve) and finds another war entirely: one with the more conservative members of the Army who still believe in WW2 tactics. Based on the author's own experiences as a young officer.

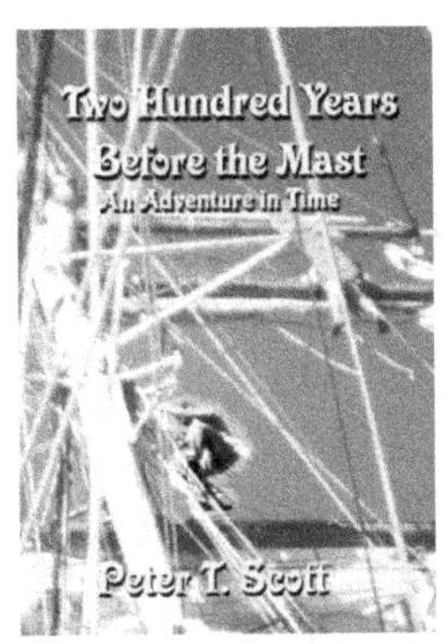

Two Hundred Years Before the Mast – An Adventure in Time is a science fiction novel. The year is 1996 and a young Nuclear Physicist accidently discovers how to travel in time. Having an interest in the 'Days of Fighting Sail', he goes back in time to the year 1796 where he is unexpectedly press ganged aboard a Royal Navy frigate bound for blockade duty in the Bay of Biscay. He realises that having a modern education is of little use back in the eighteenth-century and so he has to relearn new skills and lifestyle amongst his new shipmates until he can get the opportunity to return back to his own time. Before he does, he is able to create history as his ship battles against great odds.

NON-FICTION

Adventures in Earth Science is an in-depth, traditional Earth Science textbook on Geology, Meteorology, Oceanography and Astronomy. The latest scientific information has been given in the text including chapters on climate change and the future use of fuels and energy. The book contains over 700 pages, 1200 photographs and illustrations mostly taken by the author. It also includes 32 video links taken by the author to explain various skills as well as excursions to many exotic places in support of the text. Also has companion **Teachers' Guide** and **Laboratory Manual**.

The contents of this book have also been rearranged into the **Adventures in Earth Science Series** of eight smaller individual books in both electronic and A5 print editions.

Exploration
Science

Fossils- Life in
the Rocks

Riches from
the Earth

A Dangerous
Planet:
Volcanoes &
Earthquakes

Rocks - Building
The Earth

Changing the
Surface:
Weathering
& Erosion

Through Sea
& Sky:
Oceanography
&
Meteorology

Beyond
Planet Earth:
Astronomy

Adventures in Earth and Environmental Science is a two-volume textbook on the environment, how it is monitored and implications for the future. They come in electronic format and as A4-sized print editions with a **Laboratory Manual** for each volume and a **Teachers' Guide**.

Surviving Global Warming - A Guide for the Future is a comprehensive explanation of the natural and man-made causes of global warming with data from a wide range of reputable scientific bodies such as CSIRO and NASA. Written with many innovative suggestions for coping with the consequences of future global warming at the home, local and government levels. It comes as an electronic or printed edition.

A Pocketbook for Hiking and Survival is a concise reference book on going into the wild places of the Earth based on the author's extensive experience as a hiker, caver, geologist, Infantry Officer, ski instructor and leader of several youth groups. Topics include basic equipment, food, water, shelter, rope work, navigation and communications. The book is designed to be carried in pocket or backpack to where mobile phone signals may be lost. It is available in Kindle format as well as paperback and it is recommended that mobile phone users install it as a stand-alone document.

A Pocketbook for Surviving Teaching & Instruction is NOT an academic text on Education, but rather a sometimes-light-hearted guide to the art of teaching with some asides for instructors in the corporate or industrial world. Written in a simple, easy-to-understand manner, it would be suitable for parents wishing to know more about the teaching profession, especially if they are involved in home schooling. The text has been illustrated with some of the author's cartoons, with a chapter on the use of such art in the classroom.

All of these books are available in electronic format for any PC or tablet in Kindle format which can be read on any device using the free Kindle App. Or as print editions. Available at all Internet book outlets or from **Felix Publishing** by contacting them at:

info.felixpublishing@gmail.com